27571

248 710

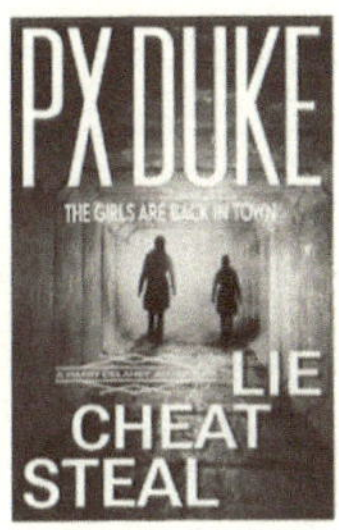

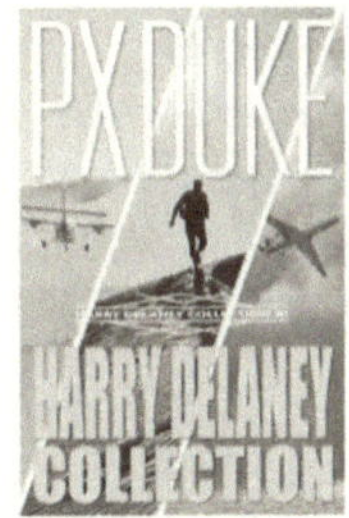

Check out all six books of the Harry Delaney Adventure series. Learn why Harry makes his way from the North African desert to the Mexican Baja. Discover how he ends up having a triumphal return to the deserts of North Africa.

Jim Nash Read Order

Marina Mystery	*Startup Blues*
Twisted Sisters	*Last Stop to Nowhere*
Sleeping with a .45	*Revenge is Justice*
Pirate Cay	*Escape*
Thrill Kill Jill	*Wedding Bell Blues*
Greetings From Key West	*Breakdown*
Lost Paradise	*Little Girl Lost*
No Angels	*Forget Me Not*
Mexico Gamble	*All The Glitter*
No Picnic	*Mexico Time*
Fallen Angels	*Partners in Crime*
Vendetta	*Shop Till You Drop*
A Girl's Best Friend	*LOBO*
Dead End	*No Free Ride*
No Harbor	*Gone*
Dog Days	*Stealing America*
Dead End	*Blame It on Djibouti*
No Harbor	*No Escape*
Dog Days	*Trouble in Paradise*

SEASONAL

Trick or Treat
Helping Santa

JIM NASH INVESTIGATES

Snap Brim Fedora Caper
The Lady in White
The Lady in Yellow

Print books

Jim Nash

Jim Nash The Beginning
Gun Crazy
Gun Crazy 2
Gun Crazy 3
Fallen Angels
Last Stop to Nowhere
Revenge is Justice
Escape / Forget Me Not
Wedding Bell Blues / Breakdown
Mexico Time
No Free Ride / Gone
LOBO
Stealing America
Blame It on Djibouti
No Escape
Trouble in Paradise
Nash & Delaney Collide

Harry Delaney Adventures

Dead Reckoning
Lie Cheat Steal
Uncharted
Go-Around
Sand Storm
Harry Delaney Collection

Frank Ross Biker Tales

No Way Out
Bad Girls
Bank Robber Dames

Other

The Last President

GO-AROUND

PX DUKE

Harry Delaney Adventures

Dead Reckoning
Lie Cheat Steal
Uncharted
Go-Around
Sand Storm
Harry Delaney Collection

For those we lost along the way.

1

Meeka **Williams checked** the car across the street through the sheer curtain covering the front window. It was a sedan, with its engine idling. Four doors. It was difficult to see into the car through the tinted side-windows. She eased the curtain aside for a better look.

It appeared as though two men in the front were gesticulating. There was no one in the back. Her father and Barbara, her step-mother, had left about an hour ago. She was certain the car had not been there then.

There were only two houses on the country street. Hers, and that of Harry Delaney. The car had to be waiting for her father, or for Harry.

Meeka released the curtain and left the front-room window. She checked the lock on the front door before retreating to the kitchen, where the clock confirmed she was right about the time.

She grabbed a chair from the table and slid it beneath the cupboard over the refrigerator. Climbed up and reached for the hidden weapon. Took it down and set it on the counter. Located the box of shells and put four shells in her left pants pocket. She kept four out.

The sawed-off shotgun and its well-worn, soft leather strap were very familiar. Her own mother had made sure she knew how to use it properly. She smiled, recalling how her own mother had put a shell into a single chamber. Demonstrated how to shoulder the weapon. How to place her feet and lean into position.

Her own mother insisted she aim the weapon at another person only if she intended to pull the trigger.

Do not worry about the target for now, her own mother told her. *We will work on hitting it later*.

She had pulled the trigger as instructed. The intensity of the explosion shocked her. Almost knocked her over. Would have, if her own mother had not shown her how to plant her feet and to lean forward into the weapon. It had also helped that her own mother had wrapped her arms around her and braced her.

Meeka put away the memory of her mother and her upbringing in the East African desert and went to the front closet. She found her summer poncho and pulled it over her head. It had rained overnight. The poncho would keep her dry on her walk through the bush. It would do double duty to conceal the familiar weapon she would hang on her shoulder.

Satisfied, she broke open the action and loaded both chambers with 12-gauge shells. She closed the breach, hung the shotgun on her right shoulder, and covered it with her poncho. She reserved two shells between the fingers of her left hand. Using her right hand, she hooked a strand of jet-black hair behind her ear.

It is time.

She left the house through the back door. Closed it and made sure to lock it behind her. She crossed the patio and made for a familiar path. It ran through a sparsely wooded area that backed onto her home. The grass was damp from last night's rain. With each step, her shoes got wetter. The trees and bushes she walked under and through were still wet. She brushed against branches. Water drops splattered onto the poncho.

She swiped at her forehead and the growing perspiration.

The shortcut brought her to the street in front of her house, perhaps fifty meters distant from the strange car. Beneath the hot sun wisps of steam rose from the street still wet from the rain.

She crossed the street and walked toward the car. Kept to the sidewalk on the same side of the street. Careful to keep the old shotgun concealed. The car's back bumper had a car rental sticker pasted on it. Two men were visible in the front. Both their shirts were bright colors of some kind.

She casually made her way past the car and disappeared from sight. Satisfied she had gone far enough, she turned to retrace her steps on the opposite side of the street.

Meeka swiped a hand at the sweat on her forehead. It would do no good to have it flood her eyes.

Her breathing increased. Became short and sharp as she grew even with the unknown car. She pivoted toward it. Made a beeline for the car's driver side and halted. She took up a position that afforded her a view inside. The two men in the front seat had so far ignored her. That was good. They didn't see her as a danger.

Meeka knocked on the back-seat window and stepped to the right of the rear door. If the front door opened in a hurry, it would miss her. The front window hummed on its way down. In one smooth motion she tossed the poncho over her shoulder to reveal the shotgun. Leveled it. Pulled back both hammers.

The men straightened immediately. Their heads did not turn. She surmised they knew such a sound well.

"Who are you and what are you doing in front of my house?"

The men remained remarkably calm. Both pairs of hands moved to the steering wheel and the dash, respectively. They appeared familiar with the position.

"I think we are lost." The thick accent sounded Mexican, but she wasn't certain. It could be Spanish. "We are looking for Mike Williams. Do you know the name?"

Meeka didn't answer. Instead, she ordered the man to unlock the back door. It clicked. She pulled it open and got in. The shotgun didn't waver an inch from her targets. "You will start the car and turn into the driveway ahead of you with the big garage door. The one on your left. Do you see it?"

The driver nodded.

Meeka continued. "After you turn, you will halt and shut the car off. You will throw the keys out of the window. Do you understand?"

The man nodded again.

"You are a long way from Hawaii with those shirts, are you not?"

The men ignored her question.

"Go."

The driver started the car and steered into the driveway. Gravel crunched beneath the tires. The car halted and the driver tossed the keys out the open window.

Meeka opened the door and hurried out of the back seat. The old sawed-off shotgun's twin barrels never wavered from their intended targets.

"Get out of the car on the driver's side. When you are both outside, close the door."

Meeka took another swipe at her sweaty forehead with the back of her left hand and then moved back to survey the operation.

The second man struggled to comply as he stumbled over the middle console. He joined his partner. Both men stood at attention, side-by-side. Their eyes never left the girl.

"You will pull up your shirts and turn around, please."

The men did as she commanded. "Gracias."

One man's eyebrow shifted up a bit. She was right.

"Now then. One of you. Walk to the door and ring the bell. The other will stay here. Do it now and then return to join your friend. Do you understand?"

Meeka, familiar and more than comfortable with the well-used shotgun, moved off to the side. If she was forced to discharge the short-barreled weapon, it would not endanger anyone standing behind the door.

2

The front doorbell chimed inside Harry Delaney's house.

Sasha, his wife, asked, "Are you expecting anyone?" She went to the front window overlooking the driveway. A car she didn't recognize was parked at the foot of it, just past the sidewalk. She noticed Meeka immediately. She didn't recognize the two men.

Sasha called to her husband. "Harry. It's Meeka. She has the shotgun. There's trouble."

Harry moved to the peephole. "I see her. Get away from the window."

Sasha backed away. "There's a strange car in the yard. Where's Ziv?"

Ziv Frakter lived in the small house behind Harry's place.

"She's at the hangar, helping the guys with the new jet."

Sasha rushed to the kitchen and the MAC50 pistol Harry had only moments ago demonstrated. She opened the box and dumped the contents. Nine millimeter cartridges clattered onto the table. Some rolled onto the floor.

She began stuffing rounds into the empty magazine. She finished. Didn't know how many she loaded before ramming the magazine into the grip. She started on the second magazine. Managed to get at least five cartridges home. She tucked the spare into her bra and headed for the door.

The doorbell rang a second time. Harry approached the door and called to the girl. "I'm coming out, Meeka." He opened the door wide.

Sasha stood in the door at her husband's side. The MAC50 hung down at her thigh. She knew it to be the last place people thought to look. But for these two. Two pairs of eyes moved to pick up the handgun immediately.

Sasha had eyes on Meeka. She stood off to the side. She recognized the familiar double-barreled cut-off against the girl's shoulder. Her left hand cradled the fore-end. She held two spare cartridges separated by a single finger.

Meeka was leaning forward, with her feet braced. She was in a firing stance.

Who are these men and why is Meeka covering them off?

Quietly, Sasha said, "Harry. Meeka has the shotty."

"I see her."

The man on her left addressed her. "Madame. You carry the MAC50 very well."

A foreign accent. Mexican? He sounded Mexican.

"It does have one peculiarity, though," he added.

Sasha's brain raced. Had old acquaintances from their Mexico days returned to haunt them? She brought up the automatic. Allowed the handgun to drift to the left of the speaker. Fired a round into the ground. Neither man moved a muscle.

"I am familiar with the peculiarity." She allowed the pistol to drift back down to her thigh.

"She's a hell of a shot with an AK, too, gentlemen." Harry looked the two men up and down.

What the hell. Something isn't right. The shirts. The Hawaiian shirts.

A flicker of recognition crossed his face. "Iván? Jofre? What on earth are you doing here?" Harry stepped through the doorway and rushed down the steps. "You can stand down, ladies. These two are my old comrades, Iván Campos and Jofre Leon."

Meeka moved away. Sasha took a step back, ready to slam the door shut on the strangers. She had her daughter Christa to worry about. It would leave Harry outside, vulnerable and on his own, with the strange men. Meeka's shotgun would certainly even the odds. She knew the girl's capabilities well.

She addressed the girl. "Meeka. I think Harry knows those two from somewhere. Come up here with me, please."

Harry guided Iván and Jofre out of the line of fire. The two men might be former comrades in arms, but until Meeka was certain, she would not stand down. The men would be formidable adversaries.

"What brings you here? How did you find me?" Harry asked.

Iván gestured to the shotty, still pointed in his direction but aimed at the ground. "The young lady discovered us, I am afraid. She is good. We flew in looking for you. Then we saw Mike's sign over the hangar at the airport. We changed tactics because we couldn't find you. We scouted out Mike's house first thing. It would seem—"

"You're here now. That's all that matters. Come in. Come in. Welcome to my home."

Sasha called to her daughter, Christa, to come downstairs to meet a couple of her father's old friends. She joined her friend, Meeka, and together the pair watched over the men as they shook hands and laughed at old jokes known only to them.

Sasha said, "Harry. I just texted Barbara. I'm going to take the girls and meet up with her. Mike will join the party shortly, okay?"

Jofre and Iván were good with that. So was Harry. "Man, is Mike going to be surprised when he sees the two of you. I have so many questions, but I'm going to wait for him to get here."

The two men exchanged glances. "That is all right. We can tell the story two times, since it will no doubt change."

They laughed.

Harry shrugged. He finally remembered to introduce Sasha and the girls before they said their goodbyes. Harry pulled Meeka aside. "Be sure to tell Mike he has to wear his Hawaiian shirt, okay?"

Meeka broke the shotgun and retrieved the shells before turning it over to Harry. He waited for the girl to acknowledge his request before allowing her to join Sasha.

Harry said, "Come out to the patio, guys." As he led the men through the house, he set the shotgun on the kitchen counter. "What would you like to drink?"

"We quit drinking, but have whatever you want, Harry. We will watch and enjoy." The two men laughed and Harry explained he, too, no longer drank. He left to return with a tray full of colas and ice. "Who would have thought we would be such a boring crew after all this time?"

The three made small talk while they waited for Mike to arrive. Harry interrupted them to put in a call to Sammy Pollard to invite him to the party. "Be sure you wear your old Hawaiian shirt, Sammy. I have a surprise waiting for you."

Talk turned to Jofre's embarrassment at being caught out by Meeka. "She is the spitting image of Mike from what I can remember, Harry. She is tall like her father for her age."

"Yes she is. And she's almost as good as Mike is, too, as you found out."

3

After Sammy and Mike showed up, the men found themselves alone on Harry's patio. All five had been fed and watered and told so many true lies and stories that conversation and laughter began to lag.

Harry finally posed the question nagging at him since his former comrades arrived.

"All right, guys. What's going on? I don't think you showed up after all these years to consume bad Canadian fruit and croissants and listen to lies about our history for the sake of the women we're married to."

Jofre took the lead. "You know we wouldn't be here if we didn't have good reason, Harry."

Iván nodded knowingly. He looked across at Jofre, who said, "We have a proposition for you, of sorts. It involves—"

Mike held up a hand. "I think I already know what it involves." He looked across at Harry before going on. "It involves going back to Africa. There's no other reason for both of you to be here."

Harry said, "I thought you guys were happily married with kids and businesses to run. Did your wives chase you off, or what?"

Iván grinned. "Not exactly, my friend. We got their permission first, of course."

They all laughed, and Harry interrupted. "Mike and I know all about that, for sure."

Iván continued. "Two of our former squad members got in touch with us about six weeks ago. Maybe a little longer. Did either of you read about those fake gold bars and the cash that landed in Zimbabwe?"

The hair on the back of Harry's neck stood up. He and Mike knew exactly what Iván was referring to. They had discussed it at length in Mike's back yard over barbecued steaks and baked potatoes the same day they read about it.

Jofre reached for Harry's picture of the group taken in the back of the DC-3. "Look here." He held out the photo. "Two died of natural causes. Another two in car accidents. And two sitting in Entebbe with eyes on the old terminal building." He let the photo fall back on the table. "Remember that?"

Harry looked at Mike and back at the two men. He remembered the building well. He had brought in a lot of goods through Entebbe, thanks to another friend who was now retired in Frankfurt. The city had been the point of origin for much of those goods.

Iván spoke up to shed light on the details. "All of us were happily retired from the business, Harry. Jofre and I have small cantinas and patios 15 or 20 kilometers apart in small towns in Spain. How the men found out, I do not know, but they showed up with their families. Later, we would all get together, sometimes twice a year for old time's sake. You know, to tell lies and have a few laughs remembering our younger days."

Iván hesitated, and Jofre took over. "We were careful. No names. No places. No dates. You know how that can be. And you never hired men with visible tattoos, for obvious reasons. None of us had a chance of being recognized for that. But still—" Jofre looked from Mike to Harry. "There is something going on. That is why we came. We want to know if you would be interested..." The man's voice trailed off.

Mike's question was obvious, but he didn't ask it. He didn't have to.

"Jofre and I thought hard about coming all the way here and finding you. We felt it was the only way to make our point."

Mike said, "And your point is?"

Jofre exhaled. "There will be at least two more flights before the fake gold and the good cash dry up."

Harry looked across at Mike, who was already looking at him. "We'll let the women sleep without worry. You two return to your hotel. Tell us where you're staying and we'll come by first thing in the morning. This needs more discussion."

When the men left, Mike brought up the devil in the details. "Our wives will kill us for sure and take the life insurance."

Harry didn't doubt it for a minute. "True."

"Barbara is pretty settled in her lifestyle."

Harry sighed. "You think Sasha isn't? Our kids would have to be flown up north to a bush camp with Ziv first thing."

"There is that." Mike thought for a minute. "No. Wait. Why, if Barbara and Sasha stay home? We'd be better off taking Ziv with us."

"Yeah, and that would go over like a lead balloon with those two."

S asha quietly closed the bedroom window overlooking the patio. Her hands went to her hips as she addressed Barbara, Mike's wife, and her best friend. "Those bastards. They want to go without us. Can you imagine the nerve?"

"They haven't said yes yet, dearie."

"I wonder how much cash Iván and Jofre are counting on?" Sasha hesitated. "Do you think it could be worth it?" She opened a dresser drawer and rummaged through it before finding her passport and holding it out. "I have a year left. What about you?"

"We got them around the same time, remember? Does that mean we're going?"

"I know one thing we're *going* to do. We're *going* to be crashing that breakfast meeting or my name isn't Sasha Delaney."

A fter the men departed, Mike said good-night to Harry. He crossed the lawn and entered his house through the back door. He was careful to close and lock it. He checked the front to see that it, too, was secure. Satisfied, he went into the kitchen and ran a hand behind the refrigerator to find that Meeka had replaced the old shotty and the box of shells. He climbed the stairs and walked down the hallway to his daughter's room. He listened before knocking on the door.

"Yes, father? What is it?"

Mike entered and sat on the edge of the bed.

Meeka set aside the book and looked up at her father.

"You did a good job today. Your mother would be very proud of you, Meeka. I am very proud of you."

"She taught me well, did she not?"

"Yes. She did."

4

A chime sounded. Mike checked the hangar's video feed. He recognized Iván and Jofre and buzzed them in. He waved to the pair from the door of his second-story office and called out. "Put your phones in that tin box at the foot of the stairs and close the lid."

The men did as they were told and Mike directed them to the conference room. They climbed the stairs and entered the room. Mike closed and locked the door behind them.

The pair took in the room. Knocked on the heavy teak table that ran its length. Raised their eyes to framed photos of what appeared to be adventures in the sand they hadn't been a part of. Recognized other photos of neat rows of tents and familiar faces.

Jofre gestured at a photo of a woman with long, dark hair hanging out the cargo door of a Twin Otter. One engine was running. There was a huge cloud of dust behind it. "Is that who I think it is?"

Harry laughed and came to stand beside the men. "Don't tell Mike you like that one. One of his survey pilots snapped it at a grass strip outside Mombasa. Sasha and I were headed for parts unknown at the time. When he finally figured it out, he met us in Djibouti. We had his daughter on board. Surely you remember her."

Mike called out from the front of the room. "She's the girl that got the drop on you." He paused. "Two of my employees will join us in about an hour. You already know Sammy. The other is Bill. Harry and I trust the two of them implicitly. Are you all right with that?"

"Well, we have worked with Sammy. We know him and trust him, too. As for Bill—" Iván looked at Jofre. "We have no choice. If you trust the man, we must as well."

"Bill is as good a tinsmith as you'll find anywhere. In another life—"

Harry interrupted. "We don't need to talk about that now, Mike. We need to find out where we are with this plan."

Jofre opened his backpack. "I have more information." He removed several aviation charts and maps and aerial photos. He unfolded them on the huge table in front of a whiteboard.

Harry broke open a felt pen, went to stand by the sideboard, and addressed the group. "What have we got so far, gentlemen?"

One by one, Harry listed the maps and charts of the region on the whiteboard as Jofre presented them. "Who are the two on the ground and on-site?"

He and Mike had wondered that very thing last night after their visitors departed. If the wrong men were there, that would kill this crazy scheme right out of the gate. The trip would have been for nothing.

"You know them. Edouard Viza is from Iván's squad. Carlos Borrajo was a member of mine. Both are good men. As you will remember, we worked with them for years with no problems."

Jofre vouched for the pair, too. "Iván is right, Harry. You know them. They're good men."

"All right then. As for our two men, you know Sammy. Bill will be along shortly, but I think I can say without a lie that Bill is very reliable as well. He came along on one of our operations and proved his mettle by rigging a couple of .50-cals to hang outside the door of our old DC-3. It worked like a charm, with Sammy's help."

Jofre and Iván appeared satisfied with Bill's qualifications.

Harry went on to some specifics. "First, I think you should get rid of your car and the rooms and move in with Mike and with me. You can tell them you're returning to wherever you came from. I'll clear it with Sasha later. And remember, we haven't told our wives about this little treasure trip. If they find out before we're ready to leave—"

Mike agreed with Harry. "They'll hang all four of us alive, believe me. And Meeka and Christa will help them." He paused. "Now then, guys, to continue with our logistics. Sammy and Bill are stripping the interior of my newest long-range jet as we speak. You probably walked by and didn't notice. We need it as light as we can get it for a trans-Atlantic ferry flight. I won't be going into details about re-fuel stops, destinations, and anything else until we're en route. Are you okay with that?"

Harry checked off two more items on his white-board list. He circled *Phones*. "Does anyone know if our cell phones will work on the continent?"

A key slid into the locked conference room door. All eyes shifted to the door. It flew wide and banged against the stop. Windows rattled.

"Oh shit." Harry looked at Mike.

Sasha strode through the open door and nudged it with an elbow. It banged again. Barbara walked in behind her, pushing a tray piled high with food and drinks. There were at least half-a-dozen boxes as well. The smell of strong, fresh-made coffee and baked bread wafted through the room. Sasha said, "I heard that, Delaney. Hello Iván. Hi Jofre. It's nice to see you again. How has it been going so far?"

She didn't give anyone time to answer.

"*Oh shit* is right, gentlemen. The cats aren't away any more. Your cell phones won't do duty on African soil. If we end up in Nairobi, or NBO as you so fondly call it, there's an entire street dedicated to them. If we go through Djibouti, we can get them there. In the meantime, we went and picked up some local burn phones. Begin charging them now and they'll be ready for later in the day. If you're smart, you'll start using them as soon as you can."

Barbara pushed the cart to the front of the room beside Harry. "Brunch is served, gentlemen. If you don't like it, you and Mike and your two friends can cook your own from your tents in our back yards."

Barbara regarded Harry's white-board. "Aren't you missing a few things? You know, destination, for one. And funding. Where is the money for this pie-in-the-sky operation coming from? Mike?"

Harry lowered his gaze and shuffled his feet. "Well, truth be told—"

"Yes, please. Do tell us the truth while you explain how you were going to make good your escape without us. Like jackals in the night, by any chance?"

Iván and Jofre snorted.

Barbara said, "As for you two 'seasoned pros', you allowed a girl to get the drop on you. I expect you will let our daughter know how good she is while she apologizes for her actions. Meeka is very possessive of her father and step-mother and will let nothing happen that could hurt either of us. She is pretty protective of Harry's family, too, since he's the one who found her and got her out of Africa."

Iván and Jofre nodded.

"One more thing." Barbara turned to address Mike and Harry. "Is Ziv coming along on this shit-show? If Meeka and Christa are coming, Ziv most definitely will be in attendance."

Harry looked at Mike and shrugged. "It looks like we've been caught out, Mike. We're going to be taking our families on an

African sight-seeing excursion to all the big game parks. Whether we like it or not."

He turned away from the group and wrote *Funding* on the board. "I have a bit of cash and a small amount of bullion stored away in a Nairobi bank vault. If it's still there, we're good to go and then some as regards funding."

Barbara retrieved a scanner from the lunch cart, turned it on and began walking around the room, looking for listening devices. "Where are your phones, gentlemen?"

"They're in a tin box downstairs. Are we good up here?"

"So far as I can tell."

Sammy unlocked the conference room door and strolled in with Bill. Sammy took in everyone before his gaze moved to the white-board.

"I could be wrong, but it looks to me like we're going on safari one more time. Preparing the new jet for a long ferry flight is coming along nicely. We'll have web seating for all. Some space for sleeping. The washroom will remain intact, as will the cooler. Ziv is helping.

Iván and Jofre exchanged glances and then looked at Sammy. "You knew about this already?"

"That's my job, lads. I get paid to keep my bosses happy." He tilted his head toward Mike and Harry.

"And your bosses thank you for that, Sammy. Before you go, there's something Harry and I need to talk to you about."

5

The big jet lifted off from the Gander fuel stop and climbed out over the Atlantic with Mike and Harry at the controls behind the locked cockpit door. On reaching altitude the engines dialed back and the plane leveled.

Jofre and Iván were side-by-side in the web seating. "We must be at cruising altitude. Did you see what they took out of this thing? Leather and woodgrain discarded on the hangar floor. It made our old DC-3 look pretty sad by comparison.

"We were definitely part of a poor man's crew back then, weren't we? How times have changed for all of us, Iván. For the better, I am certain."

Ziv Frakter got up from her seat at the rear of the plane and walked forward past Iván and Jofre. She scanned each of the passengers as she walked past. She halted at the cockpit door and her lips moved.

Jofre said, "Do you see that, Iván? She's talking to someone."

Ziv unlocked the cockpit door and opened it wide. She walked back to approach Iván and Jofre. "Meeka has instructed me to let you know you can go up and check things out. One at a time, of course. The door will stay open until we are ready to land."

"Meeka? You mean Mike," Jofre asked.

"Mike. Yes."

"Where will we be landing?" Iván wanted to know.

"I am not at liberty to say. I know as much as you do."

The men exchanged guarded looks. "I am thinking that woman is not your standard flight attendant, Iván."

"Yes. I, too, noticed the bulge beneath her jacket," Jofre said. "She looks—"

"Israeli, I would say, going by the accent."

The men exchanged glances before getting up to go to the cockpit.

Ziv opened her mouth to say something but then changed her mind. She kept her eyes on them just the same.

"She called him Meeka, Iván. It must be a nickname." Both men appeared confused. "That's his daughter's name."

Ziv caught up to the two men. "One at a time por favor, hombres." Both men returned to their seats.

Up front, Mike reassured her. "It's all right, Ziv. I think we know if they wanted to, they'd have the plane by now."

Immediately, Mike noticed the look on Ziv's face. "You know what I mean." It would be over Ziv's dead body that anyone took this plane. Mike looked at Harry.

"They're confused, Harry. You better take Ziv back and explain things."

Harry left the jet's First Officer seat and followed Ziv to Iván and Jofre. "Listen up, you two. Meeka's mother couldn't pronounce Mike's name properly. Thus we have his daughter named Meeka. Ziv can't pronounce it, either. Well, she can, because she practiced. Meeka convinced her that Mike is pronounced Meeka. So there's all that."

The two men shrugged and looked around Harry into the open cockpit. Iván said, "As long as you and Mike are happy,

Harry. So, do you both tap the giant glass screen showing up in the modern panel?"

Harry waved the men toward the cockpit and grinned. "Mike does. Old dog, new tricks can't be taught, you know?"

Mike reached to tap the altimeter, and Harry looked at Iván and Jofre and shrugged. "Don't let the man fool you. The same goes for him."

Iván turned to take in the woman who had allowed them access to the cockpit, albeit one-by-one until Harry showed up. "Who is she? I don't think she is only a flight attendant, you know?"

Jofre and Iván hadn't been introduced to Ziv before the flight left. Harry convinced Mike it would be better that way. "We can pass her off as the attendant. They don't need to know more than that."

"That's Ziv Frakter. She'll stay with the girls when we get to where we're going. And you're right. She's more than a simple flight attendant. If you ask her nicely, she will show you where things are while you're on board for the ride."

Iván left the cockpit to return to the rear of the plane. He took a seat opposite Ziv. "Your sidearm. It is not a large caliber. It can't be. The plane is pressurized."

"You are right, Iván. It's a .22 Long Rifle." Ziv reached beneath her jacket.

Removed the firearm from its holster under her left arm. Her jacket parted. Iván's eyes widened. A second pistol revealed itself tucked into the woman's belt on the right side. The position would allow her to draw both handguns at the same time.

"Yes. I carry two." Ziv checked the safety before dropping the magazine. She cleared the action and caught the cartridge before handing the Beretta across to Iván. "It cannot be a large-caliber weapon, as you correctly surmise."

Iván accepted the small-caliber weapon. "I have heard stories concerning this model. It is a good handgun. Reliable. It is difficult to come by these days."

"You are right on all counts. Very reliable. And very safe in a pressurized environment if the shooter knows her way around." Ziv reached for the Beretta, and Iván returned it.

"How do you like working for Mike?"

"I do not work for Mike."

Ziv chambered the loose round. In one smooth action, she released the slide, rammed home the magazine, clicked on the safety, and replaced the Beretta in her shoulder holster. She closed her jacket, checked her watch, stood up, and walked to the cockpit.

She leaned in. "You must return to your seat, Jofre. We will be landing shortly."

Jofre left, and Ziv closed and secured the cockpit door. She waited for Jofre to belt in before returning to her seat at the rear of the cabin.

Jofre leaned across the aisle to Iván. "Did you see that? Ziv knows where we're going. How else would she know when to send me back?"

The jet's wheels kissed the runway asphalt and braked.

Mike contacted ground control and received directions to the fixed base operator, or FBO. He turned the jet for a quick return to the departure runway before shutting down. He exited the cockpit and addressed the passengers. "I made arrangements for fuel. There's a small coffee shop and washrooms in the building. Take your time. We won't leave without you."

Ziv positioned herself to lead the group into the building.

Jofre grinned. "Come, Iván. We might as well go while we have our own personal bodyguard to clear the waiting room for us, n'est-ce pas?"

Neither man witnessed the hint of a smile on the woman's face.

6

Mike **motioned for** Jofre and Ziv to approach. "Our Frankfurt caterer will replenish food and refreshments. They'll be cleaning out the refuse tanks, too. When they arrive I need you both to check out what's being put on board before we depart."

Harry had made plans with his old friend Don Dewalt in Frankfurt, but he never knew whether there could still be some hiccups before they got airborne.

Jofre got it, but he wondered about Ziv. "Understood, Mike. I will explain to her."

"There's no need to explain anything to Ziv. She's in on everything Harry and I do. We'll be going direct JIB. Unless we're discovered, I doubt there will be problems." Mike walked off.

Ziv turned, and Jofre noticed the bulge in Ziv's jacket. She caught him looking and used her upper arm to nudge the firearm back into position. She took pains not to reveal her second sidearm.

"Are you ever without that, Ziv?" Jofre asked.

"No. My job is protection. I take it seriously."

Jofre nodded tersely. "We will be taking on arms and ammunition here, thanks to a friend of Harry's he made in a previous life."

"It appears you all have previous lives. I would never have known. No one here ever talks about anything like that."

"It is for the better, I think. Even with your job you must understand that."

"Yes. I do understand."

Barbara returned from the cockpit, where she had been in deep conversation with Mike and Harry. She approached Jofre, Iván, and Ziv. "We're going to remain overnight. There's been a slight problem with our re-stocking. Until we resolve the problem, we'll move the plane into the hangar. We'll be sleeping there, too."

It was a setback for their schedule. The crew in Entebbe would be wondering where they were and whether they backed out at the last minute. Radio silence, as it was called, was in effect until they landed in Entebbe.

Iván sighed. "Our guys on site will be wondering what's going on."

Harry attempted to address his concerns. "We can't move until we have the goods. You know that. There's nothing to be done."

"I guess it's not so bad, Harry. There will be no prying eyes to see what's going on behind closed hangar doors. It's a setback for sure, but tomorrow will be a new day."

The jet was backed into the hangar. The huge sliding doors groaned and closed on their tracks in front of the airplane. Harry and Mike called the group to assemble on board.

Harry spoke first. "I apologize for the delay in proceedings, but it is unavoidable. I'm assured the refurbishment will take place sometime this evening, if not sooner. The goods are en route as we speak. Mike?"

"I have nothing to add, other than Ziv is handing out souvenirs. On the outside, they look like cheap trinkets for when we cross the Equator. It was common back in the old days to commemorate the occasion. The medallions break down into two one-ounce gold bullion coins. If anyone gets separated and needs to fund a trip to a friendly country, that should cover it. Lose them at your peril. No matter what happens, they are yours to keep."

Mike paused, anticipating questions. There were none. "As to our ETA into our next destination, flight time will be slightly less than seven hours. That's the best I can provide until we're airborne."

While the group commiserated, Ziv opened the airstair and Sammy and Bill deplaned, unnoticed by the group. Ziv secured the door and joined the group.

Iván looked around inside the aircraft. "Sammy and Bill aren't here. I thought they were coming with us."

Harry said, "They've gone on ahead. There is a lot of preparation required before we can depart our next stop for our final destination. Some of you already know where that is. I would appreciate it if you didn't talk about it. Any more questions? No? Good. Chinese has been ordered. Let's hope the food arrives before our so-called refurbishment. Enjoy."

Ziv unlatched the door and engaged the airstair. "You're free to come and go as long as you remain within the hangar."

Immediately Jofre and Iván made for the two small doors into the hangar. The men wheeled office chairs into place before taking up their positions.

Mike grinned. "Just like old times, right, Harry?"

Harry frowned. "Yes, it is. Minus the distractions of these confounded women and children we're forced to put up with."

Barbara and Sasha responded in stereo. "We heard that, Delaney. Watch your back."

"See what I mean, Captain Williams? I think it's time for some downtime with the kids."

Meeka and Christa spread a blanket on the hangar floor beside the airstair. They produced a Monopoly board and handed out tokens as Harry sat down between them. "I haven't played this game for ages. Wait! I get the top hat! Who rolls first?"

Mike busied himself doing a DI, a daily inspection, on the jet. He moved from the mains to the nose gear as Barbara separated from the group and approached her husband. "Where is the money coming to fund Harry's hair-brained expedition? Our private bank accounts certainly can't float it. As for our business—"

Mike raised a hand to cut her off. "It's not only Harry's expedition. It's mine, too. As for the money to fund it, that bank vault in NBO is in both our names. I don't know how much he's got in it because I never cared to know. All I can tell you is that he was skimming cash off the top to fund it."

"Skimming off the top of what, Mike?"

"You don't need to know. Neither does Sasha. Have you talked to her about that?"

Barbara shook her head. "No."

"Good. Keep it that way." Mike wondered if she would. The women had been best friends even before he and Harry met them on the Mexican Baja. If anything, their friendship had deepened over the years of husbands and kids and houses and everything else that went with marriage.

A buzzer sounded over Jofre's door. Everyone looked to him as he stood to the side and eased it open. A driver handed over boxes of food and the door closed. Jofre grinned as he turned around. "Dinner is served, mes amis."

Mike welcomed the distraction. He would use it to talk to Harry about his wife's questions. At least, he would if he could grab the man's attention away from the Monopoly game he was noisily winning.

7

The monotony was broken by the arriving food. Once it had been consumed, some played cards to pass the time. Others grabbed much-needed sleep on the mesh bench seating inside the jet. For those who couldn't sleep, nerves frayed, thanks to the waiting. Some showed annoyance at being delayed. Even Iván and Jofre were becoming short-tempered.

Iván approached Harry. "Everyone is getting restless. Anything from your supplier? Shouldn't you have news by now?"

Harry shook his head. There was no news to share. Neither phone call nor text had come through on Harry's burn phone to announce a reason for the delay. To avoid further queries, he took his shaving kit and went into the washroom. He splashed cold water on his face. While he was shaving he questioned his own motives.

Both his and Mike's families were on the hook in a dark hangar in a foreign country, waiting for a shipment of arms from a man he hadn't seen or been in touch with in years. While it was true Don Dewalt had been a reliable supplier in former times—

He finished shaving and toweled off. A final look in the mirror told him he needed a haircut. Now that he thought about it, all the miscreants in the hangar needed haircuts. The women too.

Harry's phone pinged as he left the washroom. He flipped it open to find a text from an unknown number.

Don needs you to proceed to CargoFretSud. It is a short walk from the hangar. There is trouble. Be cautious.

The text was signed *Natalia*. He frowned.

Don't wife. But she didn't say what the trouble was. Customs? Police? Thieves? Hijackers? All of it? He decided not to text back to ask. The warning was enough.

Harry called to his men. "Jofre. Iván. We need to chase down Don. There are small arms and ammunition in plastic bags in the jet's lavatory."

The two men went to arm themselves. Harry called to Mike and the rest of them. "I got a text from Don's wife. I'm going to take Iván and Jofre and try to chase him down. He's not far away, according to the message. Mike, do you have a problem remaining here with Ziv and the rest of them?"

Iván returned and handed off a handgun to Harry, who tucked it into his belt.

"No, I think we're good. But we need to get it in gear. This hangar won't be available to us forever. We need to load and go as soon as we can."

Ziv broke up the Monopoly game and shepherded the girls into the rear of the jet's cabin. She hung a blanket to give them a measure of privacy and handed out pillows. Satisfied, she returned to her station at the foot of the airstair.

Barbara called to Harry. "Take this just in case. It's ready to go." She handed off the shotgun and a handful of shells. Harry hung the shotty on his shoulder.

Iván pointed to an airport map on the wall. "CargoFretSud is a short walk out the side door."

Harry nodded. "Understood. Let's go, gentlemen."

The idling two-ton truck's throaty diesel gave away its position. As if the noise wasn't enough, it was parked beneath a bright overhead light, illuminating the interior. Harry gestured to the men to approach the truck on both sides. He recognized Don's reflection in the truck's huge side mirror. Blood streamed down the side of his face.

Harry called to his men. "Trouble. There has to be someone else in the truck. Maybe even in the back. I'll take the front. You two take the back. Don't shoot unless you have to."

Harry rolled under the truck. Got up and straightened at the passenger door. Yanked on the handle. Aimed inside.

Dewalt's whisper alerted him. "Three in the back. Be careful."

Harry eased his way along the bed of the truck. Halted at the end. Waited. Peeked around the corner. Jofre and Iván were standing with their arms raised. Their handguns were on the ground in front of them. Three men surrounded them.

Harry stepped away from the truck. He pulled back the dual hammers on the sawed-off. Jofre and Iván stiffened noticeably. They had heard that sound only days before.

"Drop your weapons and get on the ground," Harry ordered. "Do it now."

Jofre and Iván used the confusion to move out of the trap. A man with a heavy German accent said, "You will not shoot. You will make too much noise."

With Iván and Jofre out of the way, Harry was afforded a clear shot at the men. "And you will make no noise at all when I am done. Do what I tell you and shut up."

The men dropped their weapons.

"Get on the ground. Now."

Iván pulled zip ties from his belt and secured their hands and ankles, then wrapped them with duct tape. He taped their mouths, too.

The ingenuity of Iván and Jofre never ceased to amaze Harry. "All right, guys. Into the back. I'll ride shotgun up front." He grinned a shiteater at the two men. "I've been waiting all my life to say something like that."

Harry climbed onto the truck's step, opened the door, and got in. "Let's roll, Captain Dewalt."

Already Iván and Jofre were busy in the back of the truck. Nails screeched against wood as pry-bars did their job and the wooden crates surrendered their contents.

8

Don **Dewalt backed** the two-ton up to the hangar's garage-door entrance and honked the horn. Ziv and Barbara ran toward the sound. Barbara hit the switch to activate the door. It groaned up on its rails and halted. The huge truck backed into the hangar beside the jet. Brakes squealed. She hit the button a second time, and the door descended. "It's about time. Where the hell have you been?"

Iván and Jofre tossed the tarp aside and jumped down. "We need help to unload. All you have to do is hand the goods down."

Barbara, Sasha and Ziv climbed up and began handing off the weapons. AKs, MP5s, magazines and boxes of ammunition followed. When the truck was empty, they pulled down the tarp and jumped off. "We're good. Let's go." The women ran to the jet to help the men load.

Harry handed over an envelope to Don. "That should more than cover it. Thanks for your help. I'm pretty sure we won't be needing anything more."

Don slipped the fat envelope into a back pocket. "It's been a slice, my friend. But you need to know I'm retired now. When my phone says Harry Delaney is calling, I'm going to hit *Refuse.*" He grinned.

Harry chuckled. "I wouldn't doubt it for a minute. Thanks for all the years of help. Mike and I really appreciate it."

"You got paid. I got paid. It's all good, old friend. So long."

Barbara raised the garage door and glanced at Don. "Do you want me to take care of that cut before you go?"

"Thanks, but the wife will handle it." Don waved and drove off into the night.

Mike called to his wife. "See if you can find the switch for the double doors, dear. We're going to start engines in the hangar. And don't worry. I'll wait for you." He grinned at her.

"The women on board that tin can wouldn't leave me behind for anything, dear husband. And Sasha, Christa, and Meeka would skin you alive when I couldn't."

Mike climbed the airstair and walked through the cabin. "Are you getting the goods secured, First Officer Delaney?"

"Doing my duty, Captain. In case you haven't noticed, everyone is a lot happier."

"Good, because all we have for the next seven hours are familiar, tired faces and some bread and water with a bit of meat thrown in for good measure. Tell our passengers to close all the blinds and keep them closed until we get airborne."

Barbara found the switch for the hangar doors. She flipped off the lights before hitting the button and the doors groaned open. Airport lighting penetrated the night. By the time Barbara climbed aboard and Ziv closed and secured the airstair, Mike had number one started and was working on two. When the start sequence ended, he advanced throttles and taxied the jet out of the hangar.

Harry settled into the right seat as Mike made the taxiway to the active runway. "Cargo secure. We're ready to go, Captain Williams."

"In that case, file a flight plan for CAI so we don't arouse suspicion."

Harry ground-filed their flight plan over the VHF radio. "Confirming Cairo, Captain. What's your ETA into JIB with all those fancy computers?"

"A little less than seven hours to Djibouti, give or take."

Harry looked across at Mike in the dim cockpit lighting. "Give or take?"

"Yeah. Give or take one engine due to fuel starvation. We've picked up quite a load."

Harry dialed in JIB on the flight controller before turning and grinning out the side window. "A pilot can't get away with anything thanks to these damned modern glass cockpits."

Mike caught his reflection against the night and grinned a shiteater right back. "Yeah, these fly-by-night schedules end up forgiving a lot, don't they?" He leaned forward and tapped the altimeter.

Harry reached to free the magnetic compass from its stowed position on the forward window post. The compass illuminated to show their heading. He shook his head. *The more things change, the more they remain the same.*

Tower frequency advised they were number one. Mike straightened the jet on the runway. He applied takeoff power. Harry's left hand covered Mike's right over the throttles.

"And away we go."

9

Djibouti ground control cleared Mike to proceed across the field to park beside the Twin Otter hiding between the hangars. His survey crew had dropped the plane off earlier in the day and departed for an R&R in Italy. Bill directed him in beside the Twin Otter. As the wings overlapped, the jet's port engine quit.

Satisfied with his directions, Bill gave the *Cut engines* sign by slashing a flat hand across his throat. Harry turned to Mike. The grin on his face was huge. "Your ETA was spot-on, Captain. Fuel starvation on number one confirmed. Even Bill didn't notice, you talented bastard."

"Back in the old days, that would have been a firing offense if it happened in the air."

Harry chastised him. "Yeah, and the old days are long gone, partner. Besides, when has any of our fly-by-night operations ever resulted in anyone getting fired— Oh, wait, there was Pantyhose Ed. And Bryn with a y. And probably a few more I've forgotten about."

Mike turned to Harry. "Funny you should mention the old days. Have you looked out the window since we arrived? You're back in Djibouti where you started."

Ziv opened the cabin door and deployed the airstair. Hot, dry and dusty air flooded the cabin.

Mike unlocked the cockpit door and exited to address the passengers. "Welcome to Djibouti, friends and neighbors. Our taxi will be along shortly. Jofre? Iván? Did you happen to notice any deux chevaux in the parking lot?" The four men broke into laughter.

Barbara looked at Sasha and the women rolled their eyes. "The four of you are something else. The last time we were all here, the Yanks were only a dream in someone's eye. Now the place is chock full and overrun with them, from what I've read."

"That's exactly what we want," Harry said. "Give us a hand stocking the Twin Otter, will you?"

Jofre and Iván made for the parking lot. Their movement didn't go unnoticed.

Barbara said, "Where are those slackers off to? We'd like some help. It's hot and muggy out here."

Harry nudged Mike. "It sounds like the women weren't expecting bad-hair days in the desert."

He turned to address Sasha and Barbara. "Meeka and Christa will help you delicate flowers if you're desperate. Mike and I need to talk to Sammy and Bill."

Bill halted the noisy two-cylinder cart by the jet's door. He and Sammy jumped off to greet everyone.

"The mount is almost ready," Sammy said. "We couldn't complete it until the goods arrived, and it arrived a couple of hours ago. It's looking pretty good. In all my years, I've never seen anything like it. We're lucky to have Bill to help."

The women finished loading the cart. "Take us to your leader, Sammy. What did you get us for lunch?"

Harry said, "I'm sorry, people, but we can't leave the plane. You'll find out why when you get a look."

Meeka and Christa chose that moment to unload one of their bags and make an announcement. "We saw your old picture with the shirts in the back of the plane. Mom and Sasha let us pick something for all of you. Would you like to see?"

"Of course we would. Do you think you could wait until Iván and Jofre are back?"

The girls grinned. "Oh yes," Meeka said. "We have something special for them, too."

Bill circled the make-shift golf cart around the Twin Otter. He halted at the cargo door. He parked as best he could to block the view of anyone trying to see what was going on. Stacked boxes helped to obscure the view.

"Okay," Bill said. "We're here. I'll give you a hand to load. Watch out for that mount. You might get hurt if you fall against it," he warned.

"Can we move it out of the way?" Barbara wanted to know.

"No. It has to be hard-mounted."

Meeka and Christa carried the lighter bags of empty magazines for the AKs and the MP5s and handed them off to the grown-ups, who positioned them inside.

"Will we have to load the magazines, Mom?" Christa asked. "I remember how to do it from the last time we were here."

Sasha, her mom, smiled and said, "I think we have plenty of time for that. Look. Here comes Iván and Jofre."

Two ratty-looking, noisy deux chevaux driven by Jofre and Iván screeched to a stop beneath the wing of the jet. "We have food and refreshments, everyone." They looked around. "Where did Harry and Mike go?"

"They'll be back in a minute," Ziv said. "They went to the tower."

Sasha walked around both sides of the Twin Otter's tail. "Where's the registration? Are you guys using the old Mexico trick?"

As if on cue, Sammy propped a step-ladder against the tail. "We did. And I want Meeka and Christa to christen the old girl. Yellow and black. Remember the old Ministry of Natural Resources paint schemes? Well, we got us one of those airframes with updated engines. She's light as a feather and will take off on a dime."

He handed Christa a small can of paint and a brush. "Do you two think you could do the honors and paint over the stencil? It's already taped for you. The other side is waiting for Meeka."

Christa looked to the top of the ladder. "That's high. Mom."

"It's all right, dear. I'll help you both."

10

Meeka **and Christa** made sure everyone had a shirt. "They're Hawaiian, just like the picture in the back of the plane. We picked them out special before we left home."

Jofre grinned at the girls. "Well, Iván. We can't disappoint them, can we?" The men donned their shirts before loading everyone into the two deux chevaux. "It's not the most comfortable rental, but it's the cheapest we could find. Allons-y! Let's go."

The old cars creaked and groaned and complained all the way to the familiar hôtel near the Place Menelik, where Jofre and Iván halted the vehicles. "Recognize the place, mes amis?"

Harry got out and cast his gaze across the street to the gelato shop. It looked good, nice and white and almost shining in the early morning light.

An older woman walked out of the shop to check the commotion across the street. Harry's men in their multi-colored shirts were getting out of two cars. The woman looked twice before beating a hasty retreat inside the shop. "Yasmiin! Yasmiin! Harry is here. Come and see."

Harry overheard the woman calling out Yasmiin's name. He walked across the street to the well-kept shop with its white-washed walls and gleaming windows. A small patio fronted the building.

Meeka and Christa remained in front of the hotel, unsure what to do. Harry turned and called to Meeka. "I need you to translate. My Somali and my French is not so good these days. You come too, Christa."

Meeka and Christa held hands and looked both ways before crossing the street together.

Yasmiin recognized Harry instantly and she ran to him. Her arms surrounded his waist as she hugged him close.

Meeka translated the girl's rapid-fire French. "She thought she would never see you again. She thinks of you almost every day. She wants to tell you about Kari."

Christa's ears perked up on hearing the woman's name. "Dad, is that the Kari you told us about? Are we going to visit her? Will she want to come home with us?"

Harry ignored his daughter's entreaties about his former girlfriend.

"Meeka, tell Yasmiin we will go to see Kari tomorrow, okay? And ask her where I can find some flowers."

Harry reached into a pocket for cash to pay for the flowers. Yasmiin shook her head and replied in French. "C'est n'est pas nécessaire. It is not necessary. We still have much of what you left for us. Tomorrow when you come we will close the store."

"Well then, Yasmiin, we will see you and your mother tomorrow, n'est pas?"

"Oui. À demain. I think my mother has something."

Her mother brushed past her and handed off two gelatos to Meeka and Christa.

They thanked her and Harry led Christa and Meeka back to the hotel. They tasted the unfamiliar gelatos on the way. "These are good," they announced, licking their lips at the sweet ice treat.

An old Citroën sedan glided to a stop behind the two deux chevaux and the engine died. As the car settled slowly on its air shocks, Harry recognized the man who got out. "Capitaine Renaud! Gilbert. Comment-ça va? Plus longtemps, n'est-ce pas?"

"Harry Delaney. You're right. It has been too long. I heard you were in town. Already the jungle telegraph has news of you and your men. Those shirts are difficile, difficult to ignore."

Harry grinned. "I'm sure you have your informants, captain."

The two men shook hands.

Renaud waved and called across the street to the girl in front of the shop. "Bonjour, Yasmiin. Make sure Harry pays in cash." A huge grin overtook his face at the memory.

The girl and her mother returned the wave and laughed before retreating inside.

"So, captain. You must be retired by now. How is that going?"

Renaud thought for a moment. "Not so bad. My wife wanted to remain, since all of her friends were here. We've been away from France for so long. You know how it goes."

"Oh boy. Yes I do. Happy wife, happy life, n'est-ce pas?"

"Oui, oui. Certainement."

"I just talked with Yasmiin and her mother before you arrived. We're going to visit Kari tomorrow. Jofre and Iván are here, too. Would you like to come with us?"

"I would be honored. Are your men in the hotel?"

"Yes they are. Mike and his wife and daughter are here, too. As are my wife and daughter. Would you like to meet them?"

"Bien sûr. I would be honored."

The crew gathered in the hotel's patio. It soon became another old home week, with stories and laughter at the absurdities soon taking over.

"You didn't have to take the hotel this time, mon ami."

The men nodded and grinned, remembering the cake-walk they had on their arrival years ago. "We talked about that earlier. We were lucky it was siesta. I think it was Iván who said your men have managed to hold it for us until we arrived today."

The men had a good laugh hearing that.

Mike addressed the captain. "Perhaps you can tell the story, Gilbert. Harry and I have left out most of the details. Besides, wives are always bored by their husbands' old stories. Perhaps the girls would like to know, too."

11

The deux chevaux were loaded in front of the hotel. Two AKs had been secreted inside the cars. Jofre, Yasmiin and her mother and Meeka brought up the rear as Iván led the way with Harry and Mike and Christa. The girl was full of questions that Harry couldn't—or wouldn't—answer until they arrived at the wall surrounding the Cimetière Européen.

Harry took Christa's hand to lead her around the wall. The girl gasped when she saw the white grave markers shining in the sun. Yasmiin and her mother took the group to the brightest of them all.

"She is here, Harry. We did as you asked. Kari's guntiino was beautiful. I gave her a pillow made with the blue and yellow dress.

Your ring is on her finger. I did not know what else to do. Kari helped us so much with the store—" Yasmiin's voice faltered and trailed off. "We come as often as we can. It is not so easy any more with les Américains. You know how it is."

"Dad," Christa said. "Why didn't you tell me Kari was so special?"

Jofre addressed the girl. "Kari was a valued member of my squad, Christa. We all treasured her and her abilities."

Iván nodded. "That is very true, young lady."

Capitaine Renaud and his wife joined the group. "She helped Yasmiin and her mother rebuild their store. I know because I watched her do it."

Christa looked up at her father. "Now I know what you meant when you told me Kari was home, Dad."

"Kari had no family but for all of us. We weren't able to be here when the Capitaine and Yasmiin brought her. That's why we had to be here today." As hot sun continued to beat down on the gathering, Harry went on. "Now it is time to return and have some gelato in her honor. What do you think, Yasmiin?"

Meeka translated the girl's response. "I think it is good that you have come here. I know it was not easy for you."

"It's all good, Yasmiin," Harry said. "There is nothing more to be done. I thank you and your family for everything you have done for Kari and for me. Now let us get some of that famous Yasmiin gelato."

He grinned at the capitaine. "Today, retired Capitaine Renaud is buying."

The group returned to the hotel. On the way, they stopped at a barber shop. When Harry, Jofre and Iván exited, they sported buzzcuts.

Mike greeted them at the hotel. "Well now. It looks like we all had the same idea." He, too, sported a buzzcut.

Everyone gathered on the small patio in front of the gelato shop. Christa and Meeka excused themselves to return to the hotel. They returned with the bag of Hawaiian shirts she and Meeka had picked out.

One by one, the girls held up the shirts. Christa said, "You can pick whichever one you want. We decided we're not a very good judge of those things, right, Meeka?"

Sammy and Bill joined the group. Even they sported buzzcuts. Christa held out a shirt for Bill. "Thanks. I feel better already, young lady." She handed off another for Sammy.

Sammy had good news to share. "Someone came through, Harry. We have the mount. We jury-rigged a sliding door.

The addition fits perfectly. Our only concern is the weight with the canisters. That thing fires so fast we'll need five or six for sure.

Harry and Mike sported a pair of shiteaters. "We'll make out all right. Are you sure on the numbers? We won't be able to find reloads."

Bill went on to explain. "If you keep the rate at 2,000 rounds-per-minute you should be good. In fact, I selected that rate for you. I made a small adjustment so it will be hard to select anything else."

Harry was satisfied. So was Mike. "Well then, I guess we're good to go in the morning."

The story-telling and laughter went on until darkness overtook the group.

Christa and Meeka helped Yasmiin clear the tables. Christa said, "Your gelato is really good, Yasmiin. I've never had anything like it before."

Meeka translated for Yasmiin. "Well then, you have at least one good memory of Djibouti, do you not?"

Harry gestured to Yasmiin's mother as Meeka translated. "I won't be coming back this way." He handed the woman an envelope. "I don't think your daughter would accept this, but I feel it is necessary for everything you have done. If you think it is too much, there are schools—"

"Oh yes. I am not shy. I will accept it. Yasmiin has chosen to go to a school on the American base. Right now, our priority is for her to learn English. After that, we will see what happens. Perhaps later she will want to go overseas to get her schooling."

Harry addressed the group as it was preparing to leave. "As your entertainment director, I have an announcement. The local theater is playing a rerun of *The Sugarland Express*. I have tickets for everyone," he joked, knowing they weren't required. "It starts around 1900 hours. Be there or be square, boys and girls."

Yasmiin and her mother tried to beg off. "It won't be in French, Harry. We won't understand it."

He smiled at the women. "Don't despair. I already checked. It's dubbed in French. I won't allow any excuses."

Mike said, "When did that makeshift theater ask for tickets?"

Harry said, "When was the last time you were here, new guy in town? They never asked for tickets then. I don't think they will now."

Christa and Meeka had never seen such a movie theater. It was outdoors, between two buildings. The sand floor was well-packed.

A white sheet hung on a wall. The projector was propped on a table, where an extension cord disappeared into a building. Rough wooden boards supported by chairs at either end substituted for seats.

Harry said, "Don't forget to buy your popcorn. You have to support the local economy in these parts."

Yasmiin turned to her mother. "I think we should start coming here with some things from the store."

"I agree, daughter, but tonight we will enjoy the movie with our friends."

12

Harry **eased back** on the yoke. The heavy Twin Otter rose to greet the sun rising over the Gulf of Aden. He radioed the JIB tower. "Spooky One is airborne and headed south. I'd like to activate my flight plan." He wondered how long it would take them to realize he hadn't listed a destination.

In the cabin, idle hands were busy loading magazines for AKs and MP5 rails. Even Meeka and Christa got into the act, supervised by Iván and Jofre. The men were all ears listening to Christa recount her story of being rescued by her dad.

"My dad helped find Meeka, too, you know. Her mother—"

Sasha touched Christa's shoulder. "That's a story for Meeka to tell, dear, just as you told our story."

Iván covered for the girl. "Where did Sammy and Bill get to? And what's that under the tarp?" A tan tarpaulin covered a bulky object by the sliding cargo door.

Jofre looked up. "Where's Ziv?"

"They all went ahead to Nairobi to organize our arrival," Sasha said. "Ziv will pick up our burner phones and paperwork for the crew. We'll hook up with them there."

In the cockpit, Mike turned to Harry. "Do we have enough fuel to get us to wherever the hell we're going? And where are we going? You never told me."

Harry consulted the glass cockpit before tapping the altimeter. It didn't budge. "We're headed to KMU. Remember that one?"

Mike knew it well. "Of course. It was a CIA strip back in the mid-70s."

"Yup. Thus the Spooky One call sign. And the dual registrations on the tail, thanks to Christa and Meeka. We can park and point in any direction and get help."

"We tried that trick in Mexico. Do you think it'll work here?"

Harry thought for a moment. "It didn't work there, but new territory, new beginnings. All I know for sure is that I'm not revealing my airport on the Kenya-Somali border until I need it, and believe me, we're going to need it on our return trip. We have friends there, too. At least, I did, the last time Sammy and I landed."

Harry reached to unbutton his shirt pocket. He pulled out a well-used black notebook and handed it across to Mike. "If anything happens to me, you're going to need that. Take a look."

Mike flipped through the notebook's faded pages. Some were wrinkled. Others were covered with coffee stains. He halted at some. Passed by others. "Holy shit."

"Yeah. And before I forget, Ziv is the only other person who knows how valuable that little black book is to all of us."

"That woman was definitely a good hire on your part. I overheard one of our comrades ask if she worked for me. She didn't answer. You know, I was thinking—"

"I was, too, but not now. KMU is coming up on the screen. Aren't these new-fangled glass cockpits amazing?"

Harry dialed in the Kismayo tower on the VHF radio. He had the Twin Otter lined up on final for a straight-in approach to the 12,000-foot runway. He punched the

VHF push-to-talk button on the yoke. "KMU this is Spooky One on 118.6." He released the PTT. "Here's to hoping someone remembers the airport's CIA background."

Harry's wish came true as the KMU tower responded. "Spooky One, cleared straight in. Fuel will be waiting on the tarmac. Do you need refreshments?"

The two men in the cockpit looked at one another. Harry pushed the talk button. "Cold water and coca would be fine if available. Thanks."

Mike left the Twin Otter's co-pilot seat and went aft. "We're going to be taking on fuel and food. Does anyone need a bathroom break?"

Christa and Meeka answered in the affirmative.

Mike returned to the cockpit and called the tower. "Would it be possible to get ground transport to the washrooms?"

"Affirmative. Stand by."

The Twin Otter had been fortunate to encounter a tailwind for the entire seven hours of flight time before Harry pulled back on the throttles. He floated to a landing and taxied to a parking spot some distance from the terminal building.

The fuel bowser approached. Mike raised the cargo door, revealing the canvas-covered package.

Sasha and Barbara moved to get out with the girls. Iván held up a hand. "I will go with them. You might get in the way. Just to be safe, you understand."

Sasha nodded. Barbara broke out the sawed-off shotgun and loaded two shells. She pocketed two more. "Consider breaking out your AK, gun girl. It doesn't sound promising to me."

Sasha tilted her head toward the cockpit. "What about those two?"

"Their job is flying this crate," Barbara replied.

Mike left the cockpit for the cargo compartment. He halted by the cargo door and removed the canvas cover. Jofre and Iván whistled their appreciation at what was revealed. Immediately they began sliding a canister toward the weapon.

"That's it, guys." Mike flipped a slider and opened the magazine. Jofre handed off the end of an ammunition belt.

"All right," Mike said. "Cover it up. If we need her, Big Bertha is good to go."

Sasha jumped to the ground to greet the fuel truck. It halted in front of the Twin Otter, where it would block their departure. She sensed right away that wasn't right. She climbed up on the driver-side running board and pulled her Glock to confront the man. "You need to be beneath that wing, partner. Move. Do it now."

She waved the Glock in the direction she wanted to go. The wild-eyed driver obeyed. He halted at the end of the port wing. "Perfect driving, dude. Now get out and go away. Fast."

Sasha stepped off the fuel truck. The man slid across to the passenger door, opened it, and ran off toward the terminal building.

"Damn. I forgot to get the keys." Sasha fired once at the cheap lock on the fuel nozzle. It broke free. She tucked the Glock into her belt before pushing a button. The gas engine popped and backfired. She pushed it again, and the pump started.

Mike opened the caps on the Otter's two tanks. "Fill'er up, woman. Leave the wing tanks empty." He grinned.

"Wings? What? There are no— Get out of here, Williams. I have a gun."

Sasha pulled on the handle to flush the fuel nozzle of dust and sand. She attached the ground wire before placing the nozzle in the center tank. "Have you seen Iván, Mike?"

"Not yet. I'll go check. If the engines start, don't stop the refuel, okay? We need as much as we can get. And whatever you do, don't forget to replace the caps."

Sasha locked the fueling nozzle and ran to the cargo door. "Jofre. Iván isn't back with the girls."

13

Iván **waited for** the girls at the restroom door. He didn't like the sounds coming from outside the building. Cars or trucks. Probably technicals in this part of the world. The locals liked them. Whoever they were.

He opened the door and pulled the Glock from his belt. He handed it to Meeka. "You know what to do. I have to use the facilities."

He finished and washed up. Splashed water on his face. Dried off and reached to take the pistol from Meeka. "I have been listening. There are sounds outside the building that make me unhappy."

Iván pushed each stall door open, looking for another exit. He looked up to check the windows. They were high, even for him. "We cannot stay here. Our help is at the plane."

The sound of the Twin Otter's high-pitched turbine engines penetrated the terminal building. "Harry must have started the engines. Walk close behind me in single file. The corridor is long. If there is trouble, you will return to the bathroom and bar the door with whatever you can find. Understand?"

Meeka said, "We understand. We will do as you say."

"Jofre will be on the way," he said, in an attempt to reassure the girls.

They had only moved a few feet down the long hall when a door banged against a wall. Iván listened, but he heard only the sound of the plane's twin engines. The door slammed shut, and he listened more carefully. He heard voices—perhaps three or four men—and they were getting louder.

Iván could not permit the girls to return to the washroom empty-handed. He pulled the snub-nosed revolver from his ankle holster and handed it to Meeka. "Up close you shoot the front sight."

"I know. My own mother taught me."

"Good. I will come to get you both when it is safe."

Meeka called to Christa. "Come on, Christa. Run with me."

Iván advanced down the long hall, clearing rooms as he went. They appeared to be offices, all empty. He checked before and after each room. Meeka and Christa were gone, but he called to them anyway. "I am almost there."

He spoke too soon. The sound of men yelling and running echoed down the hallway. There was only one way they could approach.

Iván stepped around a corner.

Five running men greeted him.

He stepped in front of them. Leveled the Glock. Fired two quick rounds. The first man went down. He fired twice more before bending to retrieve his backup in the ankle holster. Cursed. It wasn't there.

He fired twice more. Another man went down and he remembered he'd given the revolver to Meeka. He would be forced to be more careful when he passed by facing office doors.

The final two men slowed. They halted their advance and started to shoulder their AK-47s. It was too late. Iván fired four more rounds. The remaining men dropped to the floor. He walked from one to the other to confirm his handiwork. Not a man moved.

He pulled a fresh magazine from his belt and made his way to the girls. He knocked on the door before entering and called to

Meeka. "We will wait here for help to arrive."

Iván handed over his almost-empty magazine and a handful of shells from his pocket to Meeka. "Load it, please."

Meeka concentrated on the task. Finished it and returned the magazine to Iván.

"Thank you, Meeka. We are good here. No one will get past the door. I need my revolver, please."

Meeka handed it over.

Iván paused to look at the two girls.

Meeka appeared to be calm and relaxed. He wasn't so sure about Christa.

"I want both of you to sit over there. I will sit here and wait, okay? Do not be afraid, Christa. Jofre will come for us. We are safe here for the time being. Meeka, take care of her, please."

Iván took up a position in front of the door. He leaned back against the wall. Crossed his wrists in front of him. Both hands, relaxed yet ready, gripped a handgun.

No one will get past the door.

The pop-pop-pop of Iván's Glock alerted Jofre to his plight inside the terminal building. "Arm up. Iván is in trouble." He retrieved two AK-47s from the cargo hold.

He grabbed two jungle magazines and snapped them into place. He handed the second rifle to Barbara. "Let's go. Be careful. We do not want to surprise Iván."

The pair advanced side-by-side toward the building. Barbara held the door open for Jofre to enter. He gestured toward the *Washroom* sign. They approached. Looked around the corner. Spotted the bodies.

Jofre called out. "Iván! Are you here? Meeka? Christa? Where are you?"

Iván held up a palm and motioned for the girls to stay put. He slowly pushed open the door and looked out. Recognized Jofre and Barbara in their Hawaiian shirts. "We are here. We are safe. Come, girls. Jofre and Barbara are here to help us."

Iván admonished the girls to close their eyes. He swept them up and carried them down the hall past the bodies to the outside where he put them back on the ground. The sound of the Twin Otter's idling engines greeted them.

Mike waved and called out to the approaching foursome. "It's time to go, everyone. Walk around the back." He took up a position to the side of the idling starboard engine and guided them around it.

Sasha kept busy with her refueling operation.

Iván appeared exasperated when he saw Sasha was still refueling the aircraft. She acted as though nothing happened. "What the hell is that woman doing? Shouldn't she be on board?"

Mike said, "Never mind her, Iván. Sasha has a job to do just like we do. Get the girls and Barbara on the plane. We'll stand guard until she's finished."

Fuel overflowed from the aft tank. Sasha withdrew the nozzle and disconnected the ground. She tightened the fuel cap. She left the fuel nozzle locked out. Fuel flooded onto the tarmac, surrounding the plane. She called to the men over the sound of the increasing turbine whine. "Get on board! Get on board!"

The men boarded. Sasha pulled herself up behind them. She reached for Jofre's AK. Fuel continued spilling beneath the plane.

Mike looked back from the copilot's seat.

Sasha locked eyes and cranked her hand.

Mike firewalled the throttles.

Sasha jerked and collapsed against Jofre. He caught her belt and hung on to help her regain her balance. She brought up the AK, leveled the muzzle at the fuel spreading on the ground, and leaned over the payload partially blocking the cargo door. "Take this, you bastards."

Her trigger finger found the AK's selection lever and pushed it down. Satisfied, she pulled the trigger. The weapon bucked once against her shoulder. She cursed. Removed her finger from the trigger and adjusted the selection lever up a notch. When it clicked into place, she pulled the trigger a second time. A steady stream of lead punctured the fuel bowser's tank. Fuel streamed out.

Spray and pray works again.

She took in her handiwork. Fuel continued pouring out of the bowser. She aimed the AK at the concrete tarmac. Pulled the trigger. Lead landed on concrete and sparks flew. Brass bounced back into the cargo hold. In seconds, a wall of flame erupted.

Mike accelerated out of the maelstrom. "Delaney, that wife of yours is going to be the death of all of us."

"I'll take it from here, First Officer Williams." Harry's right hand covered his co-pilot's hand on the twin throttles. "Give me takeoff flaps for a full load and then some, Mike."

Mike withdrew his hand and reached to dial in takeoff flaps for a full load. There was nothing for a *Then some* flap setting in the Twin Otter's flight manual. "Flaps set for a full load and then some as requested,

Captain Delaney. We'll have to re-write the flight manual to accommodate you."

Harry released the throttles to check the flap setting. Mike's hand raced to cover off the throttles. "If everything goes to plan—"

The Twin Otter shuddered and eased into the air. It began a slow, shallow climb under Harry's capable hands. He leaned over to call to everyone in the back. "We're doing good. We have climb power. Is everyone on board?" He turned to Mike. "I should have asked that before our departure."

Mike grinned. "Practice makes perfect. You'll get it right next time, Captain. It's onward and upward for now. Oh, and I'm picturing the Twin Otter flight manual. I don't seem to recall a *Full load and then some* flap setting."

"Are you positive?" Harry asked. "I'm pretty sure I saw it in there somewhere."

Harry reached to tap the altimeter. It was instinctive, learned from years of bush flying in parts of the world most people never heard of. The rate-of-climb indicator told him everything he needed to know, but he didn't trust it, either. He tapped it, too.

"Are we going to make it to 5,000, Harry?"

It was the altitude they needed to make NBO, or to fly across to Embakasi airport.

"If we don't, I'm pretty sure Sammy and Bill will experience some measure of disappointment. And Ziv will miss her payday, too. We'll be okay. We're burning off a lot of fuel with the power settings I need to keep the old girl in the air."

Satisfied with his rate of climb, Harry turned again to look into the cargo hold. Out of old habit, he did a mental count. *Sasha. Barbara. Meeka. Christa. Jofre. Iván. Mike in the right seat.*

"Yup. The gang's all here," he announced. He slapped hands with Mike.

14

Sasha took **Jofre's** AK. She removed the magazine and cleared the chamber. Her thumb found the recoil spring lock. "Well look at that." She smiled up at Jofre. "The spring is two pieces. I pinched the crap out of my thumb more than a few times on the old spring clip. This is much nicer for a girl."

"I do not think you are a girl, madame," Jofre said.

She lifted the top cover up and looked. "This one has been cleaned. Did you do it?"

"Bien sûr. Of course. That is my job, madame." He grinned as she replaced the cover.

"In that case, thank you. I don't think we're going to be too popular at that airport on the return flight." Sasha returned the AK to Jofre. He racked to pull the charging handle to the rear before looking to see the chamber was clear. He slid the carbine beneath his mesh seat.

It was near 0200 hours. NBO, or Nairobi, was coming up on the Twin Otter's flight system GPS. Mike tapped Harry on the shoulder. "It's tidy-up time."

Harry nodded his assent.

Mike got up from the right seat and made his way into the cargo hold. His eyes roved, searching, from top to bottom and front to back. "We need to get ship-shape, boys and girls. Harry made sure to pay his way in, but don't leave anything out in the open. Jofre, that AK—" Mike swung a foot and tapped it with the toe of his boot. "Cover it, please. That goes for the rest of you. Clean this place up. And remember, we're here doing the tourist thing. We'll be visiting game farms and seeing the sights in the city. Ladies, don't forget to smile at the kind men who are going to be clearing the plane and the people into the country."

Mike turned to return to the cockpit, and then turned back. "As for you two young ladies, I trust you to ask questions when Customs and Immigration shows up. Ask plenty of questions to take the heat off the rest of us, so to speak. There'll be lots of animals to see at the game park."

"Will there be baby elephants, Uncle Mike?" Christa wanted to know.

"I'm not sure. I think the officials checking us into the country should know. You'll have to ask them, okay?"

Harry slipped the Twin onto the NBO asphalt. Ground control directed him to the tarmac in front of the local FBO, or fixed base operator. The lights dimmed. A hangar door groaned open. He adjusted throttles and slowly taxied into the cavernous hangar under the capable direction of Sammy Pollard's hand signals. Sammy slashed his throat and Harry cut the engines. Ziv and Bill waited behind Sammy.

The propellers coasted to a halt and Harry unlatched the starboard cargo door. "Welcome to Nairobi, folks. Tomorrow will be a busy day. I don't think we'll get away until the day after. If anyone has complaints, take them up with my first officer."

Mike echoed Harry's sentiment. "Harry and I have business with our Nairobi bank tomorrow. Ziv, you'll be coming with us. Bring your two friends. I think Barbara and Sasha and the girls will pay a visit to the game park. Iván and Jofre will be going with them."

Barbara opened her mouth to protest. "But—"

"That's non-negotiable, Mrs. Williams."

Mike moved to turn away and changed his mind. "One more thing. We're all going to need fresh burners. Count everyone and add two for the comrades we haven't yet hooked up with. And Bill. Don't forget about him. Sammy has arranged rooms for all of us at the New Stanley."

Both Mike and Harry had spent countless nights at Nairobi's New Stanley Hotel well before the tourist rush had started. That it had been bought out and renamed didn't sit well. It was still the New Stanley—no middle name—to them and the other members of his crew.

Sammy gave a thumbs-up. "Ziv already has the goods. And I have a van to get you there, folks. Grab your bags and follow me after you get your entry visas. The arriving officers will need your passports."

The next morning, following a late breakfast in the Thorn Tree Café, the group met in the hotel lobby.

"I've made arrangements for a tour guide to get you all to the game park. Don't forget to tip your driver, ladies."

Jofre and Iván nodded. "Pas de problème. Jofre and I will take care of that, Harry. Is there any threat you know of?"

"Not here. Not so far. My major concern is getting what I have stashed away in the bank in my hands to pay for all of this. I need Mike because his is the other name on the account. And Ziv—"

"We know why you need her. Do not explain."

"Yes, well, I hope I don't need her."

Barbara wasn't able to hear all of the conversation regarding bank details. She picked up only bits and pieces. She wasn't happy with what she heard. She walked to Mike, grasped his arm, and pulled him aside. "Michael, why are you paying for all of this? It sounds like it's going to be another one of Harry's shit shows. I'm not happy Harry is spending our money again."

Mike sighed. "He's not spending *our* money, Barbara. He's spending our money, as in his money, and my money. We worked for it. We earned it. We paid the price. We shared all the problems and the heartache and the success. He owns 51 percent of what's left in that bank. If someone hasn't made off with all of it after all these years, that is. And I own the other 49 percent."

Barbara wasn't satisfied. "Fifty-one percent? Why isn't it 50-50?"

"For the same reason he owns only 49 percent of my business back home. Someone has to be in control to make the decisions. That was our deal."

"What? I never knew—"

"That's right. You don't know."

The brightly-colored tour van pulled up in front of the hotel. The driver held up a signboard with Delaney printed on it. Harry pulled the man aside. "On the way home, make sure you stop at the Flying Club. Call it a bathroom break. Make sure you give me a call when you get there."

He handed the man his phone number and a twenty before walking off to join Mike and Ziv.

Mike said, "I saw you hand the driver something. What have you got cooked up, Harry?"

Harry couldn't hold back the smile. "Remember when Barbara called me at the Flying Club when Sasha and Christa went missing over here? No regrets about that, obviously, but you remember the Club's unwritten rule, right?"

Ziv said, "Oh-oh. What did you do? Barbara isn't in the greatest of moods." She had overheard some of Barbara's discussion with Mike.

"Nothing yet, Ziv. Your lips are sealed."

15

The game park driver was outstanding, and the tour went off without a hitch. The driver regaled the group with stories about elephants and giraffes and lions and tigers and rhinoceros. He explained recent rains had the ground covered in a bounty of green grasses and leafy trees. Small lakes and ponds held plenty of water for the animals.

Majestic giraffes grazed the tree-tops. Herds of zebras galloped. Gazelles darted. Water buffalo snorted and wandered back to their ponds. Toward the end of the tour, a baby elephant charged at the van, eliciting screams and then giggles from Meeka and Christa. Another, fully grown—obviously the calf's mother—slipped her trunk through an open window and snorted and sniffed and waited for pets and slaps before retreating.

The tour guide brought out a couple of bananas. He got out of the van with the girls and sliced them. "Hold your hand flat and let momma take the treat," he instructed.

The majestic mother elephant approached the pair, sniffing and nudging and finally smelling the banana. "Let her take it," he instructed. "Don't pull it back to tease her."

Satisfied with her banana, mother elephant used her trunk to nudge her baby toward the girls. Meeka held out her hand and the baby sniffed and then closed the tip of his trunk on the piece of banana. It disappeared into his mouth. He repeated the action until there was none left. Then he sniffed and snorted and complained with a high-pitched wail before retreating, disappointed, to the care of his mother.

The driver directed the wide-eyed girls into the van and closed the door. At the end of the game park tour, the guide asked a simple question. "Is the zebra white with black stripes, or is it black with white stripes?"

The ensuing discussion took them to the Flying Club parking lot, where everyone was ready for a bathroom break and a cool drink. As soon as the vehicle emptied and the passengers were in the club, the driver called Harry. "All went well. Your families are now in the Flying Club. It looks to be about a third full."

That was all Harry needed. He pulled the black book from his pocket, turned several pages to find the one he needed, and called the number. The bartender answered. There was no idle chatter. Harry asked for Barbara Williams straightaway.

The bartender called out the name twice. Barbara stood up and identified herself. A loud bell rang. The level of conversational buzz in the bar increased.

Barbara took the phone. "This is Barbara Williams."

"Hello, dear. Did you hear that bell? That means the next round is on you." Harry hung up, grinned, and handed off his phone to Mike. "Your turn."

"By the time we're done, we're gonna be in the doghouse for a week, Harry."

"Yeah, but that crowded dog house is going to be worth it."

Mike repeated the effort. The bartender asked for Sasha Delaney. The bell rang. The bartender announced the round as Sasha took the phone.

"Harry Delaney, you are going to pay the price."

"It's not Harry. It's Mike. And you're the one paying. The next round is on you."

That was the final straw. The bar's old-timers, recognizing the last names of the women, surrounded Sasha and Barbara. To a man they wanted to know about Harry and Mike. Were they on their way? Where had they been?

The women introduced their girls just as the phone rang again. It was Harry, asking for Christa Delaney. The bartender called out Christa's name. She held up her hand and called out "Here." The bell chimed.

"Mom. Does that mean I have to buy a round?" Christa took the phone to talk to her dad. "I don't have enough money for everyone!"

"Don't worry, honey. You and Meeka won't have to buy a single round when those grizzled bush pilots find out who you are. Just don't be shy with them and they'll buy rounds all night. Now hand the phone back to the man behind the bar, please."

Harry dialed again. It was the bartender's last call for the group.

Meeka held up her hand and replied. The bell rang one last time before the bartender hung up.

Jofre and Iván sat patiently, observing the shenanigans the four women had caused at the bar. "It looks like Harry and Mike had good times in this place. Look. There are a couple of women in the group, too. Let's go claim our ginger ales. I'm pretty sure Meeka and Christa will get a kick out of it."

The sun sat low on the horizon in the rarefied air of Nairobi when the tour van stopped at the New Stanley. Two intoxicated women, their children in tow, hopped out. Jofre and Iván herded them toward the lobby.

Harry thanked the driver and handed the grateful man an over-sized tip. "I don't think you'll be seeing that crew again. Thanks for taking care of them and thanks for your patience." He turned to the women. "So, Barbara, now you and Sasha know what happens when you page a patron at the Flying Club."

"That's great and all, Harry, but you were tasked with a mission that time when I called. This time, we didn't have anything to do but tell all those men and women where you and Mike were and what you had been up to. The way we were mobbed, I don't think we can ever go back there."

"That's exactly why Mike and I didn't come to meet you. It allowed you all to live the full Flying Club experience. Back in the day, it was the place for aviators to gather and tell lies and truths unrealized."

"There were some women flyers there, too. They were asking about both of you. They appeared quite pleased to learn the two of you were finally married and had children."

"Good to know. Now go get cleaned up, woman. We're all going dancing at the Madhouse after a late dinner."

Only Meeka and Christa didn't groan.

16

Sasha was on edge. The magnitude of what they were going to attempt had finally dropped on her. "Harry, what happened at the bank? Were you and Mike able to get the goods?" She was concerned about Christa getting bored and getting into trouble. Being locked away in their rooms and with Ziv watching over them wouldn't help in the slightest.

"Today was a bank holiday. It was totally unforeseen. Tomorrow we'll do the deed."

"Well, just so you know, Barbara isn't happy. She thinks you're spending all Mike's money. And hers, too, the way she talks. It's been going on since before we left."

Harry hesitated. "I think Mike straightened her out. He's got 49 percent of what's in that vault. I've got 49 percent of his business back home."

Sasha gave Harry a wide-eyed look. "What?" That one word was all she could get out.

"Come with me to the Thorn Tree." He took her arm and led the way, to be greeted by another old friend, the hotel concierge.

The concierge shook his hand. "Harry Delaney. It has been a long time, my friend"

"Ali. Jambo. It's good to see you. Yes it has. I'd like you to meet my wife, Sasha."

"I'll have a table for you in a minute. The usual?"

"Of course." He slipped the concierge a tip.

The concierge turned away, and Sasha looked at him. "What the hell, Harry? They're following you around."

"The New Stanley was my home whenever I was in Nairobi. It was the same for Mike and some of the guys, too. The staff took care of us. Informed for us. Fulfilled minor requests. And we made sure it was appreciated. These people saved our bacon more than a time or two, Sasha."

At the table, he pulled out her chair. "Now then. See this?" He reached for the notebook in his pocket.

"This is worth my weight in gold. No matter what happens, you must not lose it.

It contains the names of everyone I ever helped in this part of the world as well as the names of others who helped me. Some of it is coded." He hesitated before going on. "The agreement Mike and I had was that everything had to be shared 51-49. No matter what it was."

"But you never told me you owned any of Mike's business back home," Sasha said.

"I didn't see any reason to tell you. Barbara didn't know until recently. That's why I'm telling you now."

"But how—"

"All the paper is at our bank back home in a box. That's all you need to know. If, Heaven forbid, both of us aren't around, it all belongs to Christa."

"All these years. You flew captain on a Twin Otter. I know you love to fly, but why the Twin Otter? You could be on one of Mike's jets."

"Because that was what I could do best."

Suddenly sober, Sasha sat back in her chair. "That's why Mike said nothing about the Twin we stole. You know, I always wondered about that. I wondered about the jet meeting up with us in Djibouti when we brought Meeka home, too. Had it been up to me, we would have gone home commercial."

Harry regarded his wife across the table. "Now you know. It's nobody's business but ours. There's one more thing I want to talk to you about."

Sasha looked around the Thorn Tree at the locals and tourists enjoying the open-air ambiance.

Harry said, "I've been thinking of giving it all up to stay over here."

"Surely not *right* here. Isn't there someplace else you might like?"

"No. Not here," he said. "Spain. Or perhaps Portugal."

She considered for a minute. "Why those two countries?"

"It's easy to get into Portugal from Spain. It's easy to get into France from there as well. You know, in case."

Sasha didn't ask, *In case what?* "Does Mike know?"

"Yes. Mike knows." Harry knew by the shocked look that he caught Sasha completely off guard. He also knew he had to be careful. His wife had been best friends with Barbara long before they met. "I know I should have mentioned it sooner. The idea only began to form when Jofre and Iván showed up. Mike had the same idea. We came up with it separately."

"So you've talked to Mike about this?"

She was thinking about Barbara again. "Only peripherally. He has his own problems."

"But Christa—"

"Christa is young enough. It will still be an adventure for her." He smiled across at her. "It will be for us, too."

"It will mean starting all over, Harry."

"Not quite, given current circumstance. If we're successful—" He stopped there. It would be up to Sasha to make her own decision.

"What if I say no, Harry?"

He didn't hesitate. "I'll cross that bridge when I come to it."

"What if Barbara says no? What about Ziv?"

"Barbara is Mike's problem. Ziv is my problem."

Sasha frowned. "Ziv is *your* problem? How does that work?"

"I hired her and I pay her. She works for me."

"Something else you didn't tell me."

"It wouldn't be like we'd have no friends. Jofre and Iván and their families won't be far away. In fact, if we can find a place nearby with a business for you to run—" He halted, hoping he had given her food for thought.

"What kind of business?"

"That would be up to you, but if you ask me, a little pâtisserie, a bakery, would be kind of nice. With a patio. And awnings." *What did I leave out?*

"Damn you, Harry Delaney—"

"Damn us all if we don't pull this job off."

The music and the crowd weren't the same at the Madhouse. It wasn't even called the Madhouse any more. The group stayed an hour or so before returning to the Stanley.

17

Harry stared into the mirror and wondered who the man was staring back. The buzzcut of a few days ago had revealed a few more gray hairs than he cared for. He didn't even recognize the wrinkles. That wasn't surprising, though. He rarely looked at himself for more than a moment, and then only to make sure he was clean-shaven and ready to face a new day.

Well, here you are, stranger. It's a new day. What have you got to show for it?

Nothing.

Nothing beyond a crew he trusted. Bad guys. Bandidos. Except neither he nor his crew were any of the above. He considered them all to be working stiffs, just like himself. *Sure we might have been involved in activities considered illegal. But all that's in the past, well behind all of us.*

Yet here we are today.

What was this crazy notion that he could use Sasha and Christa as a distraction against the real goal of thievery? And there was Mike's family, too. They were a part of it now. When the chips fell, who would believe they were along only for the game park tour?

He needed a plan. Until he got on-site in Entebbe, he was nothing more than an observer, dependent on two former squad members he hadn't seen in years. Men he didn't know if he could still trust. And left wondering if they were working for him, or for themselves.

It's a new day, all right. New and filled with challenges.

The number one challenge was bank day. If he couldn't lay his hands on the money he had squirreled away in his previous life, all of them were up the creek and looking for paddles no one would be able to find.

He had dispatched Ziv to scout the interior of the bank. The diagram in his black book was old news. He allowed her to tear the page out of the book to use as a reference.

But that was the least of his worries. The one major stumbling block remaining was the bank boxes. Would they still be there with the gold and the cash? Or would they be emptied out by persons unknown—or more likely, crooked bank employees? He wouldn't be the first to find out the hard way.

Enough with the negativity, Delaney. It's a new day. Get your ass in gear and go meet your comrades in the café. You need them as much as they need you.

A knock on his door drew him away from his bathroom pity party. It was Ziv. "How did it go at the bank? Is it still the way I remember?"

He would be surprised if it was. Too many years had gone by with possible mergers with other local banks a possibility.

"The front house is in order," Ziv reported. "The location of the vault hasn't changed. But as far as everything else goes, it's all new. Bigger building. More floors and offices. Is that part a concern?"

"It shouldn't be. Our concern is for the vault and the boxes I'm paying for. Once we have that cash in hand—" He halted, thinking.

Ziv said, "As instructed, Sammy and I have been in the van driving the streets since we arrived. We think we can get the package, you included, straight to the airport with a minimum of fuss."

"That works for me. There's going to be one problem though. And it's a big one."

"What would that be, Harry? I think Sammy and I have it all covered. What's left?"

"We're going to need a couple of carts to get the goods from the vault to the van."

"What? How much have you and Mike got stashed down in that vault? Not that it's any of my business?"

"Cash takes up a lot of room. That's why I switched to the gold standard." He grinned at Ziv. "Not as bulky, but it sure is heavy."

"Then we're going to need Jofre and Iván, too. I was hoping we could do it ourselves. Adding two more bodies makes us pretty conspicuous if you ask me."

He wasn't asking her, but he knew better than to say so. Ziv Frakter had stood by him and Mike and their families since he had hired her. To say she was a valued, irreplaceable asset would be an understatement. Not only that, but everyone liked her. That was something these days.

He said, "I'll get Sammy and Bill to rig up a ramp for the side of the van. With four of us it should be a cakewalk to wheel the carts up the ramp and dump them. We'll toss the carts overboard and leave the ramp behind. What do you think?"

"Won't that delay us even more?"

"Do you want to walk back and forth through that bank's lobby hauling gold and cash over your shoulder in a strange country with police or who knows what else only a phone call away?"

"Sounds good," she told him, grinning. "Let's go with plan B."

"I knew you'd see it my way." Harry smiled. "Now let's go let the others know we're staying an extra day. The girls won't mind. They like being tourists. As for Sasha and Barbara, I guess I'll find out."

18

"**Mike. Did you** see this?" Harry held up a copy of the International Herald Tribune. "It's still around. In times past I liked to take a copy to Uhuru Park and sit in peace and quiet to peruse the headlines before going back to the bush."

"If you had peace and quiet in Uhuru, you're a better man than I ever was."

Harry thought for a moment. "I doubt it, but I did find a solution to the vendors wanting to borrow shillings for a cart set-up."

"You did? The harassment was almost constant. How did you manage it?"

"I'm embarrassed to tell the story now, but it was one fine near-noon. I had just settled in after a walk from the Stanley to digest a late breakfast and peruse the latest *Tribune.*" Harry halted, remembering.

"Well, don't hold back now. How did it go?"

"I was just about to flip over the first page, eager to read more news of the world, when this man approached. By then I was no tinhorn. I knew he wanted to put the touch on me. I invited him to sit down. Listened to his spiel, patient as shite as though I was god's gift to bullshitters. When he finished, I let him know he had a pretty good pitch, and he did. He was no amateur. I hesitated for a bit, just to make him sweat. And then I dropped it on him."

"Dropped what?" The same thing had happened to Mike numerous times, too.

"I asked him to tell me about the Mau-Mau uprisings."

Mike looked at him, astonished. "You did *what?*"

"You heard me. I no sooner got the words out than he stood up and scooted off post-haste. As he departed, he said over his shoulder, *We don't talk about that.* I never saw him again. He must have told all his buddies about me, because I was never bothered after that."

Meeka and Christa joined the two men enjoying the ambiance of the mezzanine while they were reminiscing over their newspapers. Christa looked at Meeka. "Do you want to tell them, or do you want me to, Meeka?"

Harry said, "Tell us what, ladies?"

"I would like to leave a message on the tree in the café," Meeka said. "Do you think that would be all right?"

"Of course it would," Mike said. "That's what it's for. Why don't you get your notebook and come to Uhuru with us? You can write it there."

"Uhuru?" Meeka's eyes widened. "That means freedom in Swahili."

"That's right," Harry said. "Uhuru Park. It's a short walk from the hotel. We'll meet you downstairs when you're ready."

Fathers and daughters strolled down Kenyatta Avenue to the park, taking in the sights as they walked. Harry thought he recognized a familiar bench that was central to the park. "We'll be on that bench when you're ready. Don't wander too far without us, all right?"

"Yes, Mr. Harry." Meeka grinned at him. "We will be careful. Sasha gave me her phone." She took it out of her pocket for him to see.

The men settled on the bench. "It's good to get away from everything, isn't it, Mike? There's something I want to talk to you about."

Mike didn't look up from his paper. "You want to be captain on the jet, don't you?"

"Yes, well, there's that, but that's not the priority right now. I've been thinking about pulling the plug."

Mike folded his newspaper and stood up. "Let's walk."

They traipsed after the girls as Harry filled Mike in on what he had told Sasha about pulling up stakes and moving to Spain. "Portugal is an option, too, but I think being near Iván and Jofre would be a definite asset."

"Those guys do get along with everyone. And it appears as though everyone gets along with them. Have you mentioned it to them?"

"Not yet. I wanted to feel you out first."

"Well, I've talked to Barbara about something similar. In no uncertain terms she let me know she's not enthused about the idea."

"Do you want me to get Sasha to talk to her? They've been besties since before we met them on the Baja."

"Yeah, no. I don't think it would be a good idea. We haven't been getting along since we landed here and she learned about your bank account. Barbara thinks it should be ours, as in hers and mine."

"Or mostly hers?"

"That too. I don't understand it."

"I don't get it either." Harry looked at his friend. "I will say this, though— Better you than me."

Mike laughed, then called to the girls.

They waved and made their way underneath the tree to their fathers.

Harry said, "How are you coming with your message, Meeka?"

"It is done. I am ready to go back now."

"She worked really hard on it," Christa said.

"I'll talk to Ali, Meeka. I think they clear the board every so often. I'll ask him if he'll do it special for us, and then we'll get a picture of you standing beside it," Harry said. "What do you think about that?"

"I would like that. Do you know if my own mother ever left a message on the board, Harry?"

"Not that I recall." He looked at Mike. "Did she ever say anything to you about it?"

"I know Eloria told me she had seen the famous tree. I think she was disappointed she had no one to leave a message to."

Meeka addressed her father and her friends. "I have my message ready." She smiled. "I will leave it for my own mother. We can go back."

"Is there anyone you want to be with you when you leave it?" Mike asked.

"I think the four of us," Meeka said.

Mike addressed his daughter. "I'm pretty sure there are more than just us who want to see you leave your message, dear. Your mom will want to be there. I think Iván and Jofre would like to be there, too. And Sasha. And Ziv." He looked at Meeka and smiled. "Did I forget anyone?"

Harry smiled down at Meeka. "Meeka, how about if you consider the four of us to start. That will make it private for you. The others could join us a few minutes after that. What do you think? It's up to you. No pressure, though."

The girl returned his smile. "I will consider it, Harry."

The foursome were almost back at the hotel when Mike's phone rang. He answered, listened, and hung up. "It's Sammy. The ramp will be ready to go in another hour."

"Finally," Harry said. "We should get the group together to go over the plan one last time."

They all met in the Thorn Tree Café at a corner table. With the hustle and bustle of people and conversation in the café, no one could overhear.

Jofre said, "Ziv isn't here. Neither is Sammy or Bill."

"That's not a concern. Ziv is with the girls. We'll go over the plan with her later tonight," Harry said. "If she comes up with any changes, we'll let you all know." He went on. "As for Sammy, his job is to get us all to the airport as fast as he can. He's been driving the streets daily to make sure he knows his way around the busiest streets that could cause us problems."

Quietly, Harry said, "There are two gentlemen at the next table paying attention to us. They're too close for my liking. I think they're speaking Afrikaans. Does anyone here speak it?"

"I had a South African squad member a long time ago."

"Tomorrow is our go day," Harry said. "I don't want to be worrying about a second front intent on hijacking our spoils of war, so to speak. We need that money. All of it."

The group got up to leave.

Iván pulled Harry and Mike aside. "When you all leave I will stay behind to follow them."

19

Iván thought it unusual that Barbara hadn't show up for the meeting. He didn't say anything, but still. Either she was on board, or she wasn't. He understood Ziv was taking care of Meeka and Christa. That was a part of her job, so Barbara should have been there. Sasha, too.

The ramp for the van was completed, and Bill had departed for Djibouti. Sammy was their driver. It was his job to get them from the bank to the airport as quickly as he could.

He didn't envy the man driving Nairobi's crowded streets on the opposite side to what he was accustomed. While he and Jofre had scouted out the downtown neighborhood on foot, a car almost clipped him when he looked the wrong way before stepping out into the street. If Jofre hadn't made a grab for him, he'd be in a hospital, or worse. He never made that mistake again.

The two South Africans paid their bill and stood to leave. Iván waited until the men entered the lobby before getting up to follow them. He made a quick stop at the hotel's tuck ship and bought cigarettes and matches He took off his Hawaiian shirt and folded it to tuck into his belt. The white t-shirt beneath was bright, but once he got off Kenyatta Street, he knew the lighting to be poor.

The men exited the hotel and turned left on Kenyatta, and then took another left onto Wabera. If they made a left onto City Hall, it would mean they were staying at the Intercontinental.

Ten minutes later they approached the Basilica. It appeared as though they were going to walk past it to the Intercontinental until they halted at a bench in front of the Basilica's covered parking lot. The men sat down and waited in near darkness.

Iván checked across the street. There was no cover there, only a few trees and a stone wall to separate him from another parking lot. He backtracked, paused, and lit a cigarette. He didn't usually smoke, but it provided a form of cover. He crossed the street and casually leaned against a tree. It wasn't the best tail he'd ever done, but it only had to be good enough.

Iván turned to scout behind him.

A young girl appeared from a shadow and slowly made her way in his direction. As she got closer he recognized her. "Meeka, you shouldn't be here."

He had spotted a girl earlier, behind him. Not recognizing her, he ignored her as just another local, or perhaps a tourist, walking home to the Intercontinental. It would be the last time he would underestimate Meeka's capabilities.

"Do not be surprised, Iván. I grew up living in the shadows with my own mother. She taught me much that I remember to this day. It is not the desert we are in, but it resembles it in other ways."

Iván silently cursed his luck at having Meeka catch him out. He was about to tell her to go back to the hotel when a van halted across the street in front of the two South Africans. Someone wearing a Hawaiian shirt got out.

The coincidence was too much.

"I have to get closer, Meeka. Stay here please."

The girl was not so easily convinced. "Come. Lean on me and we will get closer. I will be a daughter taking her drunk father back to the hotel."

Iván wasn't in a position to refuse. He lowered his head and feigned a stumbling limp. He rested an arm across Meeka's shoulders. She struggled to support him. The pair crossed the street. Iván cursed drunkenly.

There was no mistaking the voice. Worse, Meeka knew it, too. He felt her shudder as she too recognized the betrayal for what it was.

"We need to get back to our hotel," whispered Iván. "Take a left to get us away from here." He had to let the others know what he and Meeka had witnessed.

The pair turned to retrace their steps. Meeka stumbled under Iván's weight. It forced her to turn toward the intersection on which the Basilica sat. A van rounded the corner on squealing tires. The sliding door on the van opened and banged against the door frame.

The lighting was dim, but Iván was sure he recognized the van. "We need to cross the street now, Meeka. We have to see what's going on."

They were too late. Iván recognized the pop-pop-pop-pop of a small-caliber weapon. The van door slammed shut. Tires squealed. The van accelerated toward them and halted on screeching tires.

"Get in." Ziv commanded. "We're going back to the Stanley." The pair didn't dally. Iván lost his limp and Meeka straightened.

Ziv was behind the wheel. Barbara was in the back, and she was ready to tear a strip off Iván for having Meeka out so late.

"It's not Iván's fault, Mom. I saw him going for a walk and I wanted to know where he was going. Just like you did with those two men."

Iván hoped that was all Barbara wanted to do. He was convinced she had been the decoy, but beyond that, he knew nothing. He would check with Harry later.

"That's the end of the South African eavesdropping. Unless there are more of them, we should be good," Barbara said.

If he hadn't been before, Iván was convinced Ziv would neither show nor give mercy to get the job done. He would warn Jofre he had witnessed first hand what the woman was capable of doing.

20

Harry **briefly touched** on the demise of the two South Africans at the evening meeting. He announced a plan change, courtesy of Iván and Jofre. The two men had disclosed they couldn't cross the border into Uganda by land or air. He proposed a boat crossing with a small twist. Meeka and Christa would accompany the men. There was silence.

"Mike and I trust Jofre and Iván with our lives. In fact, we did that for years before we knew any of you. Both Barbara and Sasha want to keep the girls safe. If we stumble into a shootout at NBO, they'll be in the thick of it with no way out."

He halted, waiting for questions. There were none.

Ziv nodded at Harry, almost imperceptibly.

Jofre nudged Iván. "Did you see that?" he whispered. "Ziv is as big a part of this as any of us. Maybe even bigger. There is something about that woman…" His voice trailed off.

"I wouldn't cross that one to save my life. You'd better not either," Iván warned. "She was the one who got the South Africans earlier this evening. I witnessed it first-hand with Meeka. That girl is no slouch either. We learned that, too, remember?"

"You're right. I'm glad we decided to consult with Harry and Mike back in Canada about this job. It's bigger than both of us, that's for sure."

The delay was only temporary. Harry bribed the hotel's concierge to find them a camper van in good condition. He didn't let on the van would never be seen again. Meeka and Christa happily accompanied Iván and Jofre on a grocery shopping expedition to stock the van in preparation for the overland journey. They returned full of energy with happy smiles, while the two men returned exhausted by the antics of the girls.

"We must have been to every local market in all of Kenya," Iván said. "We have every measure of spice, flour, salt and I have no idea what all. Oh, and there's local chai and cinnamon sticks, and rock sugar and cloves, too."

Mike recounted the story about Harry's chai-drinking during one of their meetings with a village headman. "Harry got the glass with the dead fly floating in it. To turn it down would have been an insult. He figured the fly was boiled long enough that it wouldn't matter. So far, it looks like he was right, except for agreeing to go on this operation with all of you."

That brought a laugh as Harry arrived.

"I was just telling the guys about your fly-chai," Mike told him. "We were thinking it was good so far until you got us into this deal. Now I'm starting to wonder if swallowing that fly was such a good idea after all."

"Very funny. I just put Barbara and Sasha on a plane for Entebbe," Harry announced. "I let Sammy know they've been shipped out. We'll see them when we get there."

"The travel van is ready to go," Iván said. "We have some small weapons stashed away. Meeka and Christa have done the shopping to see us to our destination. I think Meeka is happy to be back in her element. Her

Swahili is improving daily, Mike. You should be proud of your girl."

"Thanks for telling me, guys. I wouldn't have it any other way. I'll let Barbara know, too. Oh. Before I forget. I know I don't have to say this, but I'm going to say it anyway. Clear conscience and all, you understand. We're entrusting the care of our only children to you two—"

Jofre and Iván both held up their hands. "You have no reason to say it. As you have entrusted you children to us, we would do the same with ours to you and Harry. There is no need for worry or concern on anyone's part, mes amis. Having to deal with both Barbara and Sasha is enough to worry about until we get to Entebbe. Comprenez?"

Harry waved for Christa to follow him. He led her away from the group. "Do you remember when you were in the desert with your mom? You had that tracking device I gave you."

Christa nodded. "I remember. It was pretty big. I managed to get it to work. The light came on, just like you showed me."

"Good. Well, I have another one for you. It's a lot smaller. You can wear it around your neck on a lanyard." Harry pulled the device from a pocket of his cargo shorts and held it out. "You don't have to turn this one on, dear. It's already on. I want you to wear it all the time under your shirt, all right?"

"I'll wear it. I promise. I remember that's how you found us last time."

"That's right." He gave her a small bag. "There are spare batteries and a tiny screwdriver to open the back to change them if the light stops. The light only flashes a time or two an hour. It's not like the old one."

"I'll check, I promise."

"I know you will. One more thing, dear. I don't think you should tell anyone about the tracker. If for some reason I need to find you, I'll need the signal from it."

"Not even Meeka?" Christa asked. "She's my best friend."

"I know you're good friends. I'll leave that up to you. But she mustn't tell anyone, either, Christa."

"I understand, Dad. It'll be our secret."

"That's my girl. Now give your old dad a hug because I love you."

Christa's arms went around her father and hugged him tight. "I love you, too, Daddy."

Harry and Mike inspected the back of the van before it disappeared with its occupants on the road to Lake Victoria. The cupboards were stocked with all manner of local delicacies thanks to Meeka's Swahili and her astute shopping. He was pretty sure Christa would have some of her favorite foods stashed away, too.

"Did either of you think to ask Jofre and Iván what they might like to have for the trip?" Mike asked.

"Oh yes. We shopped for them, too. They were pretty tired by the time we were done."

Mike smiled at Harry. "I'm sure they were, ladies. I'm sure they were."

"They took a break, though. They made us sit down at an ice cream place while they took turns going to a store across the street. I'm not sure, but I think the sign said *tattoo*."

"A tattoo parlor? That's strange. I wonder why? Those guys know we never hired men with tattoos."

"Are Iván and Jofre in trouble because we told? We don't want to be tattle-tales," Christa said. "They won't trust us any more."

"If I know anything about those men, you two are the least of their worries—or you will be, when they get you to Entebbe safely."

Mike and Harry traded hugs with the two girls and helped them into the travel van. "Have fun, kids. You're going on the trip of a lifetime. And the same to you, Jofre and Iván. We'll see you all in Entebbe." The men grinned and closed the sliding door.

"I sure hope that was the last of the South Africans, Harry. If anything happens to those two, my wife and yours will kill us for sure."

"Don't be so negative, Mike. They'll have to deal with Iván and Jofre first, won't they?"

"Don't be so sure about that, either. Those two are just as scared of them as we are."

The drive to Lake Victoria in the well-provisioned travel van proved uneventful. Meeka happily made injera and roti and sweet chai with cinnamon sticks and cloves and rock sugar from her mother's recipes. She hummed or sang as she did.

"Do you know what language that is, Iván?" Jofre asked.

"I'm not certain, but I think it might be Hebrew. It's difficult to tell. Singing always has different rhythms, you know?"

At the end of the first day's road trip, the men grilled chicken and goat for dinner.

While they were relaxing and drinking Meeka's chai, she regaled them with the tale of how she met Harry. "I would drive him around in the technical we stole. At first he didn't think I could drive. After I showed him, he climbed in the back with the weapon."

"He didn't need to show you how to drive?" Iván asked.

"No. It was not necessary. My own mother taught me. She showed me how to stand up with my bum against the bottom of the seat. I could see over the panel. It was bumpy sometimes, though. I would often grind the gears."

"Well. In that case, it sounds like we have our chauffeur for tomorrow. Right, Jofre?"

Breakfast consisted of omelets and Jofre's famous grilled cheese sandwiches, as he called them. The sandwiches, made with Meeka's toasted roti, became an instant sensation with the girls.

At sunrise, they broke camp and headed off in the van. Meeka was behind the wheel.

"I can fit in the seat now," she said, smiling. "And there are no gears to switch. All I must do is steer and stop."

Iván said, "I don't think we should tell Barbara I permitted you to drive, Meeka. She might not be happy."

Christa chimed in. "We won't tell anyone, right, Meeka? Our lips are sealed."

The huge grin on Meeka's face made it impossible for her to answer.

On reaching Usenge on the shore of Lake Victoria, Jofre and Iván bartered the van for a fishing boat and crew. The boat had twin engines and was capable of reaching speeds as fast as 30 knots. It came with a crew of two. The owner was only too happy to accept a tip in American dollars to take Jofre and Iván and their daughters into forbidden Ugandan waters on a tourist fishing trip.

They got off to a good start. The huge lake was calm for its size. According to the forecast provided by the boat owner, there would be no bad weather en route. Six hours into the trip, it was announced a refueling stop was needed.

Meeka hurried to tell Iván that the boat crew was planning on leaving all of them ashore after they robbed them. "They did not say anything about killing anyone. Even so, I do not trust them."

Iván called Jofre aside. "I think we need to get rid of our boat crew. How are your boating abilities, my old friend?"

"About as good as yours after spending all of our years on desert sand. I've been watching the captain. It looks pretty simple. Flip a lever to put the engines in the water. Start them. Advance throttles. Steer. What's to worry?"

Iván grinned. "You were planning on taking this boat all along."

"Bien sûr. Of course. Why wouldn't we?"

He was interrupted by the boat captain. "We will pull into the leeward side of that island."

"Where is the fuel?" Jofre asked. "I do not see it." It was beginning to get dark.

"We will roll the drums to the shore and pump it from there," the captain said.

Iván and Jofre prepared for the worst. They pulled their pistols from their bags. Checked the actions and tucked the guns into their belts. Jofre warned Christa and Meeka not to be alone with the men under any circumstance.

"Jofre, I think we should take command of this vessel after it has been refueled. Thanks to Meeka's warning, we can hold them at gunpoint leave them behind. I think they will be better off there than if they accompany us farther. We won't have to worry about a mutiny."

"I agree. Let's do it that way." He looked at Meeka. "Meeka, don't let them know you speak Swahili. We could all be in danger."

Already Meeka had donned her poncho. Iván recognized it as the one she had worn when she outsmarted her two traveling companions in front of Harry's house.

"Do you have what I think you have, Meeka?" Iván asked.

She nodded. "Yes. Barbara and Sasha insisted that I bring it. *Just in case*, they said. I will protect Christa no matter what."

"We're going to leave the men ashore after they get the fuel for the boat. Remain here with Christa, as you said. Do not come ashore no matter what happens, all right?"

"Already they are talking of leaving us behind and taking our things. They are not nice men," Meeka said.

"Good. We will take care of it. We aren't going to be stranded here, no matter what. Remain on the boat with Christa."

21

Iván started the engines. He eased the boat off the beach. An engine faltered when its propeller stirred up sand, but it caught and Iván proceeded to ease the boat around. The GPS the former captain had set up gave their position and provided the route to Entebbe. "It's all good. We're on our way once again."

Worry-wart Christa was concerned about leaving the men behind. "Will they be all right? They don't have anywhere to sleep."

Jofre smiled. "They'll be just fine, young lady. Do not concern yourself with such creatures. They would have taken advantage of us, most likely as night took over. Thanks to Meeka and her Swahili, we can be safe, and you and Meeka can get back to the kitchen." Jofre smiled again at his joke.

"My mom wouldn't be happy to hear you say that, Jofre," Christa told him. "She doesn't like men who say things like that."

"If you will recall, young lady, both Iván and I have been just as busy in the galley washing up. We have done more cleanup and washed more dishes on this excursion than any man alive. And don't forget those fine grilled cheese sandwiches both of you have come to like so much."

Christa grinned. "Well, since you say it like that—"

"Now then, young ladies. All this sitting around has made me hungry. Who's ready for a fine lettuce, pickle, tomato and beef sandwich on a croissant? Perhaps a little mayonnaise would go well, too. What do you think?" Iván asked. He winked at Jofre.

The girls said, "Yes, please," in unison.

As she leaned over the side of the boat to dip her fingers, Meeka said, "There is so much water, Iván. I have never seen so much. If only we had a little bit of this when I was with my own mother." Water trickled past her outstretched hand.

"Your life jacket, Meeka," Iván said, as he reached for her belt to ease her back into the boat.

Jofre kept watch in the bow. Iván operated the helm while he put together his sandwiches. He sent Christa forward with a plate fresh-made for the watch crew up front in the bow. He thought he could hear Meeka smacking her lips. Or perhaps it was Jofre. Or, more likely, both of them. He smiled.

Sleeping arrangements weren't practical, but Iván had rescued a couple of foamies from the van for the girls. They settled into them after filling their stomachs and fell promptly asleep. It had been a long day for both. Jofre tucked them in with two sleeping bags for insulation against the cool night air slipping down the hills.

When the girls woke from their nap, the night was pitch black. At the helm, Iván dispatched Meeka to Jofre in the bow. "You can help Jofre keep watch for other vessels that might get in our way. He might like a little nap, too. In that event, you will take over for him."

"I can do that."

"And don't forget your life jacket. You, too, Christa. And before I forget, there is one more thing you must not forget."

The girls were all ears. "What's that?"

He gestured upwards to the night sky. "What do you see overhead that you don't see in the bright lights?"

Both girls looked up to observe the bright Southern Cross beaming down on them.

Iván turned to Christa. "Would you like to steer the boat for a bit?" The grin said she was eager to try. "I'll show you what I have learned so far to help out." He pointed in the direction she was to proceed. He demonstrated pulling back and advancing the throttles. "If you suspect anything is going wrong, do not hesitate to halt the boat, no matter what."

Meeka joined Jofre in the bow.

Jofre said, "We must keep watch all around us. I read that in a book about pirate ships when I was a boy," he told her. "If you look back, you will see the red and the green and the white light glowing on our boat. They need to be turned on at night so others can safely see us and not run into us. Harry's plane has the same lights at night."

With the girls organized, the two men left them in control to go make more sandwiches for breakfast. Iván gestured to a huge glow on the horizon. "I expect that is Entebbe. I will be happy to see it, my friend."

Meeka left her watch at the bow and approached the two men. "I see lights on the water. They are coming straight toward us."

"Captain Christa." Iván called to the girl. "There is a switch on the panel marked *Lights*. Please turn it off and pull back the throttles to idle. But don't shut the engines off. Let them run at idle in case we need them in a hurry. There might be trouble approaching."

The position lights went out. The boat settled into the water as Christa did as she was told.

The men checked their pistols and spare magazines as the unknown boat drew closer. It too reduced speed. Their running lights stayed on. Iván and Jofre looked nervously at each other. This was totally unexpected. "Girls. Keep to the bottom of the boat, please. We do not know who is approaching."

Jofre said, "No one knows who we are or where we are, Iván. The men we left ashore had no means to communicate with anyone. We took their phones. How could that boat have found us so easily? It is steering straight for us."

The men pulled out their sidearms and prepared for the worst. Christa and Meeka looked nervously at each other. Christa said, "Who do you think it could be? Do you think we are in trouble again, Meeka?"

"I do not know, but you should stay close to me, Christa. It is my job to look out for us. It is the job of Iván and Jofre to do the same thing for both of us."

A female voice drifted across the water and called to the men. "Ahoy, Iván. Ahoy, Jofre. How are our girls doing?"

There was a huge sigh of relief in the darkness. Jofre said, "You can turn our marker lights on, Christa. It is your mother and Barbara."

Iván tied off the boats. The women stepped aboard and looked everything over. The freshly-wrapped sandwiches drew their attention immediately. "What do you gentlemen say to joining us on our night-time cruise to Entebbe?"

The men agreed it would be easier to admit they were on a sight-seeing trip and got lost, rather than arrive in an unknown boat with two children as passengers. The men handed over luggage and helped Christa and Meeka into the new boat.

"How did you know where we were?" Iván asked. "It's pitch black out there. It's a huge lake with far too much water for my liking."

"We never reveal our secrets, Jofre." She looked at her daughter. "We like to play our cards close to the chest, don't we, Christa?"

"Yes we do, Mom."

"All aboard that's getting aboard, mateys," Barbara announced, "and don't forget those sandwiches. It's time to make for shore. Meeka, would you like to take the helm of this contraption and take us to our final destination?"

Iván whispered to Christa.

Christa said, "I'll keep watch in the bow, Auntie Barbara."

"That's my girl."

The deserted boat was left behind to float on the waters of Lake Victoria.

Iván and Jofre chatted with the two woman as Meeka piloted the craft toward the lights of Entebbe reflecting off the low overcast in the distance.

Iván said, "We were able to go over the airport photos Harry provided. Until we can coordinate with our compadres on-site, we think we can control the target until our needs are met. There is only one road in and out. The site is surrounded by a curb that protects the highway. If we end up staying at the place you mentioned, it will provide good access and control as well."

Sasha asked, "Are Edouard Viza and Carlos Borrajo up to the job, in your estimation? It's been quite a while since either of you had dealings with them."

"We talked about that on the way across. They were good men in the past. We trusted our lives to them. Harry and Mike did, too. I don't think we will be disappointed."

Jofre said, "Our main problem is going to be the schedule. How many flights remain? Will they continue to use Entebbe airport and the terminal building? How many guards are there? How are they armed? Who is backing them up if they get time to make a phone call? Military? Local police? No matter what, we must block the only access road in and out."

Barbara frowned. "Surely your friends have all of that mapped out by now, don't they?"

"They should, yes. But Iván and I would like to confirm it." "Do you have any word from Harry and Mike back in Nairobi?"

Sasha said, "They're good to go for tomorrow. They've been sitting on their asses long enough to bore them to death. If it all goes well, we should see them sometime late tomorrow."

"Mom," Christa called. "The shore is getting close."

"All right. I'll take over." Sasha gestured to a building in front of them near the shoreline. "That's our hotel. We've got our own block of rooms and all the privacy we need. All the rooms are joined by a common outdoor area in back. It will allow us to come and go and mix and mingle as we please with a minimum of curiosity from the other guests. We also arranged tables and chairs and a couple of grills so we can do our own cooking if we choose."

"Oh, Mom! You should taste Jofre's grilled cheese sammiches. They are so good. And Meeka's roti and chai and injera are just as good."

"It sounds like all of you were on a picnic, not on a boat cruise across Lake Victoria. You're having entirely too much fun."

"The guys let Meeka drive the van, too—oops. I wasn't supposed to tell anyone about that."

Jofre and Iván grinned nervously at Barbara, unsure of what to expect after having that news revealed.

"Well, I think an adventure such as the one all of us are on deserves to be a little unpredictable. Wouldn't you say, Iván and Jofre?" Barbara looked at Meeka again. "Besides, you both got to captain a boat, too. Sasha wouldn't allow me to take the helm. I think she suspected I might drive us aground."

Meeka said, "And we were on watch, too."

"Well there you go. In that case, you have quite a story to tell when you're asked to describe what you did last summer on your vacation. Your classmates will be jealous."

22

Harry **Delaney was** having second thoughts about the scope of the operation to which he had dedicated family and friends. Already it had been compromised by two South Africans. They had to be taken care of. And he wasn't even on-site in Entebbe yet. How many more problems might there be by the time they all got there?

Part of the problem was the delay in accessing the spare cash he and Mike had locked away in two Nairobi safety deposit boxes. He had sent Ziv Frakter to scout out one bank. She returned with good news about accessibility. He took it upon himself to scout the second bank, not revealing it as a part of his and Mike's former empire. It was still in the same small bank, tucked away in another part of town.

Sammy had the van ready. He'd been driving the unfamiliar streets on the unfamiliar side of the road. He had the route to the airport aced. If traffic became a problem, he had alternate routes mapped out.

The hand-built ramp he had been constructing was ready. All they had to do was open the sliding door and slide the ramp out until it dropped to the ground. The carts loaded with Mike and Harry's payday would get pushed up the ramp and into the van. When Sammy drove off, the ramp would stay behind, left on the street.

That was why Harry never told them about bank number two. Without a ramp, there was no way he'd get the money on board the van. If he used his crew to hand-carry cash and bullion out of the bank, there would be no telling what would happen. He didn't want to get the crew into a gunfight in the middle of Nairobi. Streets, airport, bus terminals and the train station would get shut down in the event that happened.

That's the last thing they needed if they were going to hook up with Sasha and Barbara and the crew waiting patiently in Entebbe for the real action to begin.

He considered making a call to Sasha to find out how they were doing. She had sent him a short text to announce the safe arrival of the sailors and their babysitters. Mike had received a similar text from Barbara.

That was a huge relief for both men. It allowed them to concentrate everything on the cash-and-carry operation, as they called retrieving the money from the Nairobi bank.

Harry pushed back his chair in the Thorn Tree Café and stood up. "They're all safe and waiting. It's time."

Mike, Sammy and Ziv nodded. Mike said, "Yes, it is. We're long overdue to get going, Thank all of you for dedicating yourselves to this op. If we're successful, all of us will be set for life." He turned to look up at Harry.

"And if we're not," Harry said, "we'll be complaining about the food in an African prison."

Sammy said, "I tucked MP5s into the van doors. I'll be too busy driving to have one in mine. There's an AK strapped to the roof if anyone needs more firepower. The mags are loaded and taped. As far as the route goes, I've got it aced, barring any unforeseen circumstances. I think we all know that can mean just about anything on this continent." He looked at Harry before disappearing to get the van.

"All right, well, that about covers it," Harry said. "Let's get going. There's not much sense in burning daylight or flying time."

The team slapped hands, picked up their bags, and made for the hotel entrance. Sammy arrived with the van and they boarded. There was silence in the cramped quarters. Harry sat up front. Ziv and Mike sat on the ramp. Sammy obeyed speed limits and traffic signals.

Harry said, "Dammit. There isn't a place to park."

Sammy nodded. "We have plenty of time, Harry. We'll go around until we get one." He steered back into traffic, then jammed on the brakes. His passengers grabbed what they could for support as he jammed the shift lever into reverse. He slowly backed into a suddenly empty parking spot in front of the bank doors and braked to a stop.

As Harry opened the door and stepped out, Sammy grinned. "Nous sommes arrivées, as Jofre and Iván would say. I'll keep her running."

Harry proceeded into the bank. Ziv followed a short distance behind. Mike remained outside. He pulled a pack of cigarettes from a pocket of his cargo shorts and lit up. It was a perfect excuse to linger outside the bank. He coughed and exhaled. His eyes began to water and he tossed the cigarette aside. "Must be a bad batch," he remarked to a passing pedestrian, and shrugged.

He strolled up to the van and rested his arms on the open window before leaning in. "I hope this all goes smoothly, Sammy. I sure as hell don't want to get into a firefight in downtown Nairobi."

Sammy grinned. "Ziv took care of those two South Africans. Surely there aren't more greedy people besides us. Do you think?"

Mike pushed away from the window and went back to scanning the street on both sides, looking for anything out of the ordinary.

Sammy had left the van angled into the street. If anyone backed too close into the parking spot in front, he'd be able to push the vehicle out of the way and edge past. He wasn't prepared for the step-van to halt beside him. The driver and passenger both deserted the truck. "Mike," he called out. "*Mike!*"

Already traffic was backing up behind the step-van. Mike walked into the street and began directing traffic around the van.

Sammy deserted the van, got into the truck, and started it up. He reversed it and parked it behind the van. He got out and tossed the keys to the curb. He said, "We just got our perfect roadblock to get us out of here in a hurry."

He had no sooner said the words than Ziv banged on the cargo door. Sammy jumped into the back and slid the door open. It banged against the stops. He put his back against the side and put both feet against the ramp. It squeaked out the open door and landed partially on the curb at a sad angle. It was unusable in its present position.

"Dammit." Sammy got out, opened a back door, and rolled the spare tire to place it beneath the one corner to even out the ramp. Harry and Ziv arrived in time as he leveled the ramp and helped push the cart up and into the van.

Harry clambered into the van. "Let's go. Let's go!" Harry yelled. "They started asking too many questions I didn't want to answer."

Doors slammed. The engine raced. Sammy slammed the van into drive and stomped on the accelerator. He laid on the horn as the van rocked into the busy street. "Traffic looks to be normal for the time of day. We should make the airport in thirty."

Sammy jacked the van hard onto Moi Avenue. Steered around the traffic circle to take a left onto Hailie Selassie. He followed Selassie to Ladhies Road and floored it left onto Jagoo Road. "We're good on this to the old Outer Ring Road."

"Damn, Sammy. You could start a bus service with all you learned about traffic in this place."

"No thanks, Harry. The stress level would be too high and the wages too low. I'll take our payday any day of the week."

"Don't count your money too soon, old friend. We're not there yet."

Not quite a half-hour later, Sammy called, out, "Here's where it gets dicey, everyone. Brace yourself. Big bump coming up!" He steered left and the van bumped over the curb and into the Fixed Base Operator's side of the airport. Unserviceable jets were parked in every direction, with no rhyme or reason. Doors were open. Windows broken. Engine parts and whole engines lay everywhere.

"Holy crap. How long has it been since we were here last, Sammy? It looks like a bomb went off but it didn't hit anything but tin."

"We taxied here from the main runway and missed the trash parked and packed out back. I wouldn't give a nickel for any one of those airframes," Sammy said.

Ziv leaned past the van's front seats to look out the window. "Looks like some kind of security guards at the Twin. Any chance they're your personal hires, Harry?"

"No." Harry's one-word answer sparked the group into action. Suppressed MP5s were drawn out of the doors. "Don't kill anyone. We have to come back through here for fuel on the trip north. That goes double for you, Ziv."

"No worries, Harry. I have my methods." Ziv pulled a taser out of her bag, exited the van, and pointed it at the biggest of the men standing by the twin. She pulled the trigger. The man hit the airport asphalt like a bag of cement. She yanked on the leads and readied for another shot. She didn't need it. The man's friends held up their hands in surrender. Ziv looked over at Harry and grinned. "See? I can behave."

Harry's long forgotten Swahili kicked in. "Jambo. What brings you to my airplane?"

Mumbling among the transgressors ceased and one said in English, "We are here to guard the plane for a man."

"What man?" Harry asked. "Have you been paid?"

"Not yet."

"Come with me, friend." Harry walked to the van, reached into a bag, and withdrew a cache of U.S. dollars. He handed it over to the man. "See that your friends are paid. It is time for you to go. If we see you here again, you might not be so fortunate. *Kufahamu*? Understand?"

The man nodded and disappeared with his crew.

"Harry, are you going to quit slacking and give us a hand with the heavy stuff or what?"

"Yeah, sorry about that. I had to abandon the attempt for bank number two. My key didn't work. I would have had to drill the lock on the box. We'll consider it reserve for a future operation."

Ziv frowned. "What the hell, Harry. How many banks do you own over here?"

"Our operation was strictly cash-and-carry, Ziv. The more cash we could carry, the happier we were. Right, Mike?"

Mike could only grin at the remembered phrasing they used to joke about. "Tote that barge. Lift that bale. And no slacking. We have places to be and people to see, in case any of you forgot."

23

Harry started number one while Mike made sure the goods were secured in the cargo hold. Satisfied, he made his way up front to the first officer seat to discover Harry cursing.

"What's up, captain? Did you forget the start sequence, or what?"

"The starter on number two is done." He turned in his seat to the cargo compartment and called to Sammy. "We're going to need a starter-generator. You got any contacts over here?"

Sammy approached the cockpit and leaned in. "Nah. I don't need them. See that Twin over there? I'm thinking it's a parts magnet for us. Is there anything else we're going to need?"

"Nope." Harry taxied on number one to the obviously disabled Twin Otter and went through the shut-down sequence. "It's all on you, my good man. There'll be no dilly-dallying allowed on this trip."

Sammy said, "Too bad we don't have Ali here with one of his technicals to climb on."

Already Mike had the cargo door open and was on the ground. He made his way to rusted-out, paint-faded Toyota. He yanked open the door on squealing hinges, leaned in, and ripped out a wire harness from beneath the dash. He crossed more than a few wires before the truck coughed and hacked to life on the third or fourth try. He man-handled the steering wheel and drove it on half-flat tires to the junked Twin Otter. He halted the Toyota beneath number two and got out.

Grinning, he bowed in Sammy's direction and pointed both hands at the paint-faded, sad, broken-down Twin Otter. "Sammy, our chariot awaits the good graces of your tool kit and our replacement starter-generator."

Sammy handed his tool box to Mike, jumped to the ground and made for the truck bed. From there he climbed up onto the roof and beckoned to Mike to hand over his tools.

Mike smiled. "If I could I'd have Barbara here to help you, Sammy."

"No worries, Mike. She works too slow for my liking. And I don't need anyone to hold a flashlight in the daytime. Here. Take this cowling, please. Leave it in the back of the truck so I can button her up like new after I claim the part we need."

Sammy worked magic with his tools and had the starter removed in jig time. He waved to Mike to take him to their Twin Otter in order to remove the cowlings. He attached multi-meter leads to the live start circuit on number 2.

"You were right, Harry. The voltage is no good. I'll have her ready in a couple of hours max."

Ziv brought out a deck of cards and the rest of them played poker with AK-47 rounds for chips. When that got boring, they walked around the aircraft graveyard, inspecting the dilapidated airframes. Both Mike and Harry were familiar with a number of them.

"Remember that one, Mike?" Harry pointed to a broke-down DC-3 sitting on its belly. "It got our asses out of Dar more than a few times. She made us a lot of money, too. Look at her now. I'm almost embarrassed to admit I flew her."

Ziv said, "How do you know it was that one, specifically?"

Mike gestured to the barely visible registration, bleached out by the desert's blazing sun, on the vertical stabilizer. "It's small and hard to read, but believe me, we both sat up front and in back on that one more than a few times for sure." He turned to Harry. "Do you remember when we hauled ass out of Dar that last time? Which reminds me, did we ever get our money out of that bank in Dire Dawa?"

"Thanks for the reminder, Mike. And no, we didn't. It's still sitting there. No worries, though. It's not going bad any time soon."

"You two. I swear. How do your wives put up with your antics?" Ziv asked, only half serious.

Harry grinned. "Woman, if you play your cards right on this trip, you too could be the winner of an all-expense paid train ride from Djibouti to Dire Dawa and back. How does that sound?"

Ziv didn't have time to reply. Sammy called down from the Toyota beneath their number two. "Okay, Harry. After Mike backs us up and out of the way, give her a try."

Sammy climbed down and gave the signal for Harry to go through the start sequence for the Twin Otter's number two. The starter held, and number two ignited without a hitch. He went to ground idle and immediately lit number one while Ziv helped Mike and Sammy get his tools collected and the Toyota out of the way.

They climbed aboard and Mike secured the cargo door. Harry was already taxiing when Mike climbed into the right seat. "I ground-filed a flight plan for SRT," he said. "We've got clearance and we're good to go."

Ziv got up from her seat and stuck her head into the cockpit. "I don't see any maps. Where the hell are you taking us, Harry?"

Harry tapped his head and looked across at Mike before grinning a shiteater for Ziv's benefit. "It's all up here. SRT is Sorota. We can't let anyone know where we're actually going. A little diversion won't hurt. Besides, we're already late. Flying low and slow over Lake Victoria into EBB in the dark of night is good strategy. Besides, Mike and I know the area by heart. It's an old heart, but it's still good today."

Ziv turned to leave. "Before I forget, would you call Sasha and let her know we're en route, please? I won't have a proper ETA until we're at least an hour out of NBO. And find out how our girls are doing. They probably haven't stopped talking about their adventure with Iván and Jofre and the boat ride."

Mike turned to Harry. "I'm dying to find out how Meeka liked floating on top of all that water. She's never seen as much water as there is in Lake Victoria in her life."

Ziv returned to the cockpit with the news. "Everyone arrived safe and sound. Iván and Jofre were flat on their backs and resting as we spoke. The girls had quite an adventure, apparently. You were right. They can't stop talking about it. You'll be listening to the stories for weeks, I'm sure."

Mike said, "Yeah, I'm thinking those men were pretty happy when they landed ashore and could hand off the girls to their mothers."

"Oh, no. Their boat got hijacked and they had to leave the crew ashore somewhere. Apparently Barbara and Sasha took a boat out to meet them in the middle of the lake or something. I wasn't sure, and I didn't want to waste time asking."

"That's all right, Ziv. I gave Christa a tracking device to wear around her neck. Those women would have found the girls no matter what."

"They're expecting us when we get there," Ziv said. "Not one minute before."

24

It was 0200 hours. The city of Kampala and its lights were to the north. Harry turned wide over Lake Victoria. He continuously checked his radar altimeter. He monitored the terminal frequency, waiting to overhear an altimeter setting transmitted to an approaching aircraft. He picked up a transmission and dialed in the numbers. To make sure, he tapped the gauge on the glass cockpit. "Call out my radar altitude, would you? I'm not accustomed to being over all this water any more."

Mike said, "Sasha confirmed the taxiway clear and usable. The grass is clear, too." The asphalt taxiway lay beside the EBB terminal building. There was a grassy expanse where they could park the Twin out of sight and away from prying eyes.

"We're 100 over the water. 3,700 ASL. Just a bit shy of Nairobi's altitude. The old girl should slip in there quite comfortably."

Harry said, "The Canadians who designed and engineered these beauties did a good job, didn't they? I'd hire them in a heartbeat."

"Shoreline coming up," Mike called. "100 feet."

Harry pulled back the throttles on the twin turbines. Mike flicked the landing light three times. It was the agreed-upon signal to announce their arrival for the night landing they needed.

Sasha looked up from her lounge chair. Stars were briefly blacked out by the plane's silhouette. It passed over the Lido Resort just above rooftop level with barely a whisper.

She hurried into the lobby and down the hallway to knock on doors to announce the plane's arrival. Iván and Jofre quickly geared up and headed out the back door on their way across the highway to meet the plane and its passengers.

The men were all business as Mike and Sammy passed out luggage and boxes.

Ziv, who had geared up while they were still airborne, stood guard. She nervously walked around the plane, on the lookout for vehicles and nosy people eager to learn what was going on at such a late hour.

Iván and Jofre approached cautiously. Neither wanted to surprise Ziv. They quietly called her name.

She responded. "How was your boat ride with the girls?"

"It was slow but we had a good time. We made sailors of the pair of them. I permitted Christa to captain the boat while Meeka stood watch in the bow. I think they had fun, right, Jofre?"

"We all did for sure. But Meeka blew our cover when she announced Iván allowed her to drive the camper van." The men chuckled, remembering the expression on Barbara's face when she found out. "It's good to be back together, finally."

Sammy passed out the last bag of their Nairobi treasure. "All right. That's the end of it."

Iván approached Harry and pulled him aside. "Did you know there is a refinery down the street from our hotel, Harry?"

"A refinery? What do you mean? What kind of refinery?"

"A gold refinery. We checked it out late yesterday. It appears to be secure, too, from what we could tell. We didn't approach anyone or ask questions. We only scouted."

Mike looked at Harry. "That might change everything. We need to meet with Sammy and Bill about aircraft parts we can ship home. What do you think?"

Harry said, "I think if they can forge it for us, we can ship it. We have enough people here to do aircraft parts painting for sure. Now let's get across the highway. I'm tired and I want to see my girls."

The mood across the road at the Lido resort was festive now that everyone was in place. No one went to bed. They gathered beneath the palapa on the beach and everyone was caught up on what transpired during the brief absences.

Meeka and Christa welcomed everyone with hugs while constantly chattering about their camping experience and the pirates who tried to kidnap them while they were on Lake Victoria.

Harry said, "At noon tomorrow we're going to have a meeting." "I have new information that could make our final result worthwhile if we can get our hands on the goods. In the meantime, I'm off to bed. You all should do the same. Good night, everyone."

Jofre and Iván approached Harry.

Jofre said, "We have not seen our comrades since we arrived. I spoke with my wife. She hasn't heard from them either. That's who they were to get in touch with if they didn't hear from us. I told her we were on-site, but to be careful what she said to our former squad members, just in case, you know?"

"Does your wife know where you are?" Better to know now than to find out when it's too late.

"No. She does not."

That was good enough for Harry. "Surely Viza and Borrajo will be surveilling the airport to determine our target's next landing. They'll spot the Twin Otter for sure and ask questions, don't you think?"

Jofre said, "We will start our own recon tomorrow before sunup. That will give us some warning. As for our friends, well, they have to be close by. How else would they know about the planes if they are not already watching the airport?"

Harry nodded. "Tomorrow before the meeting I'm going to check out the refinery you mentioned. Maybe one of you would like to come to check out security. What do you think?"

Iván said, "I too would like to see what goes on there. If they are truly refining gold, the security must be impressive in this country. We didn't see anything out of the ordinary when we scouted, but things change so fast."

Again Harry nodded. "That they do, gentlemen. That they do."

Harry briefed Mike the next morning over a breakfast of fresh fruit and plenty of Meeka's home-made fresh chai.

Mike couldn't resist licking his lips at the remembered taste. "I wonder if I could convince my daughter to put a fly in yours, Harry? Just for old time's sake, you know?"

"Thanks but no thanks, partner. I'm good. Meeka's chai brings back fond memories, doesn't it? By the sound of it, Iván and Jofre had their hands full with the girls on that land and water trip. Two more capable men we never would have found to trust them with our children like that. I'm glad we brought the kids. It's the trip of a lifetime for them, I'm sure."

"I had my doubts, but you were right. Do you think we can actually use that refinery? And what would it cost us?"

"Well, a little baksheesh in this part of the world goes a long way. I'm wondering if the gold on those flights we're looking for might end up there to be replaced by lead. Or vice versa. If that's the case, we're going to have to have a guard or two to oversee the operation we might need to conduct."

Mike said, "Barbara and Sasha come to mind. They can do that. They ought to be tired of working on their tans by now."

"You're right. And it wouldn't hurt to have someone who can speak the language on site as well. Meeka can always pretend it's a school project. What do you think?"

"I'll run that by Barbara, but with Sasha there too, it probably won't be a problem. As long as they're armed. We'll need the security for our product, not the refinery's. It will look more professional if we have our own guards."

"Then that's the way I'll present it to the refinery's management this morning. If I have to buy our way in, I'll do that, too. It's about time we spent some of our earnings, don't you think?"

Mike agreed. "There's no better way to spend it than on more money, that's for sure."

Neither Iván nor Jofre were able to raise their comrades. In the past, Edouard Viza and Carlos Borrajo had proved to be valued members of their respective squads. They last spoke with the pair before leaving Spain for Canada and their visit with Mike

Williams and Harry Delaney. Thanks to the efforts of Edouard and Carlos, they were able to convince the two men to come on board.

They found themselves in a pickle now, without ever having put eyes on their former comrades in arms. Harry and Mike wouldn't be happy when they passed on that news.

Iván said, "Do you think someone found them out? Maybe they got into a bar and started shooting their mouths off about the huge payoff."

Jofre said, "I don't know, but I don't want to go to the police. That would be a tipoff for sure, don't you think? The last thing we need is advance warning of any kind on this job. Harry is not going to be a happy man when we tell him the men who got us to come here can no longer be depended on to help us."

"We'll be fine without them. How many flights can there be that land, taxi to where we are parked, and unload cash and gold? Even if the gold turns out to be lead, the cash will be good. At least, that's what they've been unloading the most, according to our two missing men."

They returned to the resort, where Jofre and Iván discovered Edouard and Carlos, the missing men, waiting for them. They were sitting beneath the palapa they had used the previous night.

Iván said, "We were about to give up on you, my friends. It's good to finally see you. We managed to convince Mike and Harry the payday would be a good one, thanks to your scouting abilities. They're both here, too."

"The next flight will occur in three days," Viza announced. "That is according to the airport workers we have bribed. We must be ready by then if we're going to be successful."

"What's the level of security you have witnessed so far?" Jofre asked. It would have to be substantial, given the amount of money changing hands.

"There is no security so far as we can tell. Nothing beyond what they bring with them on board the plane. No vehicles. No troops. No police. Nada. Nothing."

Iván asked, "What happens with the money? What do they do with it?"

"From what we have witnessed so far, it's loaded into a van and driven off. Sometimes the van goes to the gold refinery. Sometimes it goes into the city. From there, we have no idea."

Jofre said, "So when we hit it, it will have to be at the airport. That's good. It keeps it simple. All our resources can be dedicated to one place."

Edouard said, "We need to get back to work. Tell Harry we said hello."

Harry approached Ziv at the dinner table. "I'd like you to start sleeping on board the Twin. Do you have a problem with that?"

"Not at all. Twenty-four hours, or night only?"

Without hesitation, Harry said twenty-four hours. "I know it's asking a lot, especially since we have this nice resort hotel to enjoy. I can have Meeka bring food and anything else you want. No limits."

"It won't be a problem. Do you have word of someone planning to cause us problems?"

"Not yet, but better to be safe than sorry."

"Is there anything on board I need to be aware of? You know, in case I have to retreat."

"If you retreat, I'm going to have to steal an airplane to get us out of here. Do you see any spares parked on the tarmac?"

"I understand. No retreat."

25

Following their walk to the resort across the airport grounds, Harry and Mike came up with a simple plan. It involved striped orange vests like those worn by the airport workers, and garbage bags.

"Christa, I have a secret assignment for you," her father, Harry, said. He winked at Sasha and Barbara.

"Ohh, dad, Can Meeka come too? We've been helping each other on this trip, you know."

"If it's all right with Mike and Barbara, she can certainly help. Now then, did you bring that camera with you? That new-fangled one that prints out a picture after you take it? It prints in color, right?" Harry asked.

"Yes. I brought it. I have plenty of film left, too. And it prints in color. Iván and Jofre were getting tired of the flash going off on our trip."

"I'm sure they were. You won't need the flash on your secret assignment, though." Harry lowered his voice to a conspiratorial level. "Here's what I'd like. Airport workers all wear a colored safety vest for visibility. You remember from when you visited us at the hangar back home, right?"

"Oh yes. You and Uncle Mike and Sammy and Bill make us wear them all the time."

"In that case, we need to know the color patterns for the vests the workers wear around the Entebbe airport. They might not be the same as back home. Once we know, we can go downtown and buy a bunch. We'll need some of those pick-up sticks, too. Enough vests and sticks for everyone."

Sasha was smiling at her daughter's serious face. She looked at her husband. "Pick-up sticks? What do you mean, Harry?"

"Oh, and I almost forgot. Garbage bags. We need to know what color they use for the men working around the airport grounds that pick up the trash flying about."

Sasha looked at Barbara and the two women shrugged. "Harry, you better explain yourself."

Harry ignored the women and went on, secret-agent style, for Christa's benefit. "We'll need to pre-fill the garbage bags with trash. Something light. Maybe newspaper that's been scrunched up. The bags have to look like they have trash in them. Maybe a third or half full. No sense overdoing it."

Christa and Meeka were whispering to each other.

Ziv appeared in the doorway and signaled she was ready.

Harry nodded to her, then looked at the girls.

"Young ladies, maybe you could walk with Ziv to the plane when she goes. Let her know about your assignment and what you need. I'm pretty sure she'll be able to help if you need it. Does that sound good?"

Ziv smiled at the two girls. "The traffic drives on the opposite side of the road here so—"

Meeka interrupted. "We know. Iván and Jofre let me drive the van when we were on our road trip."

"Yes, well, you'll be walking now. This is very important. Before you cross the street or the road or the highway, you must remember to look in the opposite direction for cars coming. Which direction are you going to look first?"

Meeka's and Christa's response came at the same time. "Right!"

"That's right," Ziv assured them. "Right is right. Why will you look right first?"

"Because that is the side where the cars are driving. Where they are coming from. Right is right. Just like in Nairobi."

"Very good. Do not ever forget on pain of death."

Harry looked around the room. "Does anyone have any questions?"

Iván and Jofre ignored Meeka's comment about her driving abilities. "Genius, Harry. We'll fit in and we'll look good doing it. We're going to need coveralls, though."

"That's right, and thank you for reminding me. Coveralls for everyone are part of the plan, too. Before I forget. No one who isn't in this room needs to know anything about this, and by that, I mean Viza and Borrajo."

Iván and Jofre nodded.

There was no doubt their first day was going to be a long one. Exactly how long would depend on how much time it took for Christa and Meeka to return with the photos. Without pictures, a trip downtown would be wasted until they had evidence of vests and coveralls.

Sasha approached Harry. "I've been looking online. There's a hardware store on the highway to town. I'm thinking they'll have everything we need. About those sticks you mentioned—"

"Pickers. You know. Grabbers. Whatever they're called. So you don't have to bend down to pick up the garbage," Harry explained.

"Ooh. I get it now. You want us all to be airport employees of some sort."

"Exactly, my sweet, and you will be the prettiest one of all in those ugly coveralls. When Meeka gets back, I want her to accompany us to that refinery up the street. Her Swahili eavesdropping will more than likely come in handy."

Sasha said, "Did you know there's a bulk cargo shipper next door to where you parked the Twin?"

"Really? You are worth every penny I pay you, wife."

"Yeah, after all these years, I'm still waiting for that promised payday, husband."

"Now now, let's not be greedy."

"What's greed got to do with it? It's all about how big the pickle jar is going to be."

"I swear, between you and Christa—"

"There's no winning," finishing Harry's sentence for him. "I know, dear."

It had been a long day. The crew ate a late dinner beneath the stars to discuss the day's activities and plan for the next. "Who wants to go first?" Harry asked. "Good news preferred. The bad can come later."

Christa and Meeka held up their hands. "We took pictures of the people wearing vests. There were only two. The rest look the same. The uniforms look like they're in the army."

Mike said, "Good work, you two. And good news, too. There'll be a little something extra in your piggy banks next week."

"That's nice, Uncle Mike," Christa said. "My dad makes me use a pickle jar for my allowance."

Everyone broke out laughing and Harry's face turned red.

Sasha said, "It's true and no laughing matter in our household. "He pays me the same way." She couldn't keep the grin off her face.

"All right. All right," Harry said. "I admit it. I tore a page out of my old desert notebook and brought it home for the women in my life. Now let's get down to business. Good work, Meeka and Christa. Does anyone besides our young ladies have anything to add?"

Jofre said, "Viza and Borrajo are still trying to nail down a date and arrival time. We might have to settle for a date with an unknown time. They said it would be three days. We'll find out, I guess, one way or the other."

Harry nodded. "We still have to take a look at the gold refinery. I'd like to take Meeka and Iván and Sasha on that job. Meeka will be able to listen in on the chatter the employees will have. Are you okay with that, Mike?"

"I think so. I don't see any problems so far."

Harry said, "All right then, ladies and gentlemen. So far, we have the photos we need, thanks to Christa and Meeka and their hard work on our behalf. Ziv is keeping an eye on our plane for us. She's camped out on board. If anyone decides they might like to sneak aboard for whatever reason, don't, unless you give her fair warning. And Sasha found a hardware store of the kind likely to have vests and coveralls for us once we determine if we need them. The place is up the main road a bit toward Entebbe."

Harry paused to give the group time to digest the information. "If there's nothing to add and no questions, you're free to do as you please. The next meeting will be over breakfast."

26

The gold refinery was a quick walk away on the same side of the highway as the resort. Harry, Iván, Sasha, and Meeka were able to walk the shoreline until they got to the hotel blocking the way. At the entrance, the road switched out to the hotel and then the refinery.

At the entrance to the refinery, a locked gate and a guardhouse greeted them. Harry explained he'd like a meeting with the owner or manager. The two guards held a confab. Thanks to a whispered translation by Meeka, Harry learned security thought it unusual they had arrived on foot.

"No worries," Harry said in English before switching to broken Swahili in an attempt to explain. "Our team is taking advantage of staying at the Lido. Your business was close-by, and thus we are here to make general inquiries."

The guards went into the blockhouse and conferred before one picked up a phone.

Meeka grinned up at Harry. "Not too bad for one so not used to speaking in a foreign tongue. You did good. I'm impressed."

"You can thank all the time I spent in your part of the world for that, Meeka. But I still need you to play your part as well."

"Hakuna shida, Mr. Harry. No problem."

"I don't speak any foreign tongues beyond some misremembered Mexican Spanish," Sasha told the pair. "It looks like you're doing all right so far. They're on the phone. I'm pretty sure we'll be seeing more security and maybe even a boss soon enough."

"You are right, Sasha. They will be here soon," Meeka said. She had been listening in on the guards past the blockhouse door.

The guards scanned them for weapons before loading them into a van and taking them to the building entrance. More security greeted them in the form of armed guards.

An important-looking man in an electric-gray suit approached. "You should have called to make an appointment, good sir. I see you have brought your family with you."

"Oh, no. Not my family. These are my business partners—well, my business partners and my daughter. She is doing a school project when she gets back to Canada. It is customary to report to classmates on what everyone did during their summer vacation. Young Meeka would like to do a school report on your fine business establishment."

Harry had learned a long time ago that a little flattery would get you a long way in this part of the world. He wasn't disappointed.

"Yes. By all means. Come in and I will get my secretary to take your daughter on a brief tour while we talk business. Am I right to assume you might have some business to discuss?"

"Ndiyo. Yes. Hapo ni kweli. You are right. The girl brought her camera," Harry added. "Is it all right if she takes some pictures, too? With permission, of course."

Meeka, proud of Harry's abilities, squeezed his hand and smiled.

The secretary approached the threesome. She smiled as well.

Harry said, "Go with the lady, dear. We'll see you here when you are finished with your tour."

Iván said, "Harry, they are looking us over pretty good. I think they are taking pictures, too."

"If they bother to call the Lido to check, they'll find every word of what I said to be true. That we have most of the hotel rented will not go unnoticed. Wait and see."

The manager said, "I must go and make some routine phone calls. Stay here. I will be back shortly."

"See? He'll be back with a smile and a handshake," Harry assured his crew.

Meeka was waiting for the group in the lobby. She was chatting with a young girl. "This is the manager's daughter," Meeka told Harry. "She is learning English. Her mother brought her to speak with me."

"So then, we made an impression after all," Harry said. "Good. Now let's make our way home. I promised Christa I'd take her to the other side of the hotel to visit the aircraft boneyard."

"Still looking for some of the old airplanes entered in your log book, are you, Harry?" Sasha asked. "Don't you have enough to think about besides a tin farm?"

"Hey now. Christa asked about it and I said I'd take her. Mike is coming too. You're welcome to join us, favorite wife of mine."

Sasha looked at Iván. "See what I have to put up with?"

"If that's all you have on him, I'd say you're doing pretty good, right, Harry?"

"Don't take your life in your hands, Iván," Harry warned him. "You still have to get home to your own family in one piece."

The men grinned.

"I think they are only fooling us, Sasha," Meeka said. "Otherwise, you would not be here with us from the beginning."

"I think you're right. You should see the aircraft, too. Your father has quite a pilot's log book to go along with Harry's impressive list of accomplishments. Now let's get back."

Harry returned from the visit to the refinery at a loss for words. He was impressed with the professionalism of the operation. Security was excellent. The manager appeared eager to please. He had even allowed his daughter to talk to Meeka. Still, he wasn't completely sold on their operation.

He grabbed Mike before they headed off to the aircraft boneyard. "Are we sure we want to go through with this, Mike? I'm having doubts."

"Doubts about the refinery? If you're not comfortable, we won't use it. We'll ship it home using that freight forwarder."

"That's the thing. Where, exactly, are we going to be shipping our product to? Is it going to be our old home, or to someplace new?"

"One thing at a time, old friend. We came here to do a job. Let's get the job done before we start dreaming of new horizons. Now come on, Meeka and Christa are waiting to find out how boring our lives are."

That's pretty much it in a nutshell, Harry thought.

27

Iván's walkie-talkie activated. Static followed by a broken voice came over the airwaves. He reached to adjust the squelch before throwing back the covers and jumping out of bed. He pulled on his cargo shorts. He tucked his pistol into his belt, and hung a suppressed MP5 over his shoulder before donning his Hawaiian shirt.

On his way out of the hotel, he pounded on Jofre's door.

It opened immediately. "I heard," was all Jofre said. He too was dressed and ready to go. "I can't get an answer. Those damned walkie-talkies we bought are supposed to be first-rate, aren't they?"

"I didn't get a reply either. No matter. We will go to Ziv now and hope we are not too late."

The pair hurried out of the hotel and across the highway. Before advancing farther, they paused for a quick view of the plane Ziv had been left alone to guard.

"The plane is dark. There is no signal light as we agreed. There is trouble, I'm sure. She wouldn't call if there was nothing."

"No, she wouldn't. And she definitely would answer us if she could."

Both men shouldered their MP5s.

"I'll go left," Iván said.

Jofre moved to the right, and the pair advanced toward the Twin Otter. They were on full alert.

Iván put through another radio call to Ziv. There was no response, not even the click-click of a transmit button to acknowledge receipt of the call.

"There is no code word. Nothing. I hope we aren't too late."

The men approached the Twin Otter from both sides.

Jofre called Ziv's name as quietly as he could.

Iván did the same.

Neither received a response.

The Twin Otter's jury-rigged cargo door opened and rattled up on its rails. A dim light illuminated the interior. Inside, someone was bent over. It appeared as though someone was going through the pockets of another laying on the cargo deck.

Jofre called, "Ziv!"

The person straightened. In the dim light, it was impossible to tell if it was Ziv or another person.

Iván came up on the rear of the Twin. He stood just off to the side of the pogo stick, the jury strut that prevented the tail from contacting the ground when the aircraft was parked. His position gave him a clear view inside the forward cargo compartment in the dim light.

"It's Ziv! She's okay."

Ziv jumped to the ground and landed in the soft grass in front of the two men. "Thanks for answering my call. I'm sorry I couldn't get back to you. I was busy cleaning the mess." She gestured to the man lying on the cargo deck. "I think the batteries in that damned radio went dead on me."

"That's all right. We were only concerned we would have to deal with Meeka if anything happened to you." He smiled, only half serious.

"I understand what you are saying. Were it me, I would not want to deal with her either in that case."

Jofre asked, "What have we got here, Ziv?" "Is that who I think it is?"

Iván was already on board, examining the body. "Yes. It's Viza. And he's wearing one of our shirts."

"It has to be one he bought himself. We have no extras as far as I know," Jofre said.

Ziv began to explain. "I asked for the password and—"

"He wouldn't be familiar with it. We never used such a system when we worked with Harry and Mike in the past."

"When he didn't know what I was talking about, he reached behind himself and I thought he was going for a gun. I didn't give him the chance."

"No need to explain, Ziv," Jofre insisted. He removed the handgun from Viza's belt and held it up. "He was against us. Now he is dead. It's going to be daylight in an hour or thereabouts. We need to get the body out of here."

"I'll stay to cover you off, Ziv," Iván said. "Go back to the resort and get cleaned up and have a decent breakfast. Get some sleep. Jofre will handle moving Viza. Come back when you are ready, not before."

"That is music to my ears, gentlemen. Thank you."

Jofre hoisted Edouard Viza's body over his shoulder and began the walk back to the hotel, accompanied by Ziv. He said, "We are fortunate you found out. Now we need to learn how he has compromised our operation."

"We only arrived a day ago. He was never at our meetings. He met only with Harry and Mike, did he not?" Ziv asked.

"Yes. And they will not be happy to learn one of their own has betrayed them and compromised the operation. I'm going to leave it to you to let them know. If they ask, tell them I'm busy floating our former desert comrade to a watery grave."

Harry and Mike waited impatiently until Ziv had eaten and showered before calling the group to a meeting.

When they were all assembled, Harry said, "If you haven't already heard, Ziv had an early-morning caller. He didn't have the password. The security breach has been handled, thanks t Ziv."

Ziv said, "Iván is covering me off. I'm going to bed. If you have news for me, that's where you'll find me."

"Edouard Viza was wearing one of our shirts. It had to be obtained locally because we have no spares as far as I know. Jofre is handling him. As for good news, we have the information on the uniforms of the airport trash patrol. They are nothing more than green cargo pants and green camo shirts and ball caps. We were able to get everything we need at a local hardware store."

Harry looked around the room. His disappointment at being betrayed by one of their own wasn't lost on the group.

"Meeka and Christa are busy stuffing empty garbage bags with newspaper to make them look official, for lack of a better word. We've got pick-up sticks and gloves for each of you. What we need is for you to slowly start to pretend to pick up trash in the airport terminal infield. The area is close to where we know our target will arrive."

Mike said, "Don't all of you go out at the same time. There isn't a person that will show up on time to do that job in this part of the world. Take your time. Do it slowly. Try to make it look like just another clean-up job no one wants or needs."

Harry said, "I have a new password for you. It should be easy enough to remember. All of you have been in the back of an airplane with Mike or I at the controls when we needed to do a go-around, thus our new password: Go-around. When Ziv wakes up, have her come and see me and I'll give it to her personally. Send Jofre to me, too, when he gets back from conducting his burial at sea."

The group dispersed. Only Harry and Mike remained behind, huddled over a table.

Mike said, "Do you think any of them suspect our plan?"

"Hell, we only came up with it this morning while we worried over Ziv. Still, I think we were right to go with the trash-picking detail. Mind you, our options are limited. What else could it be that wouldn't look out of the ordinary?"

"True. If we were just standing around, it would be a dead giveaway. We need a reason to have people on-site, and that's it."

"I dispatched Bill across the field to go over the mini-gun package one last time. That's the one thing I want to be sure works perfectly. And while I'm on that subject—"

"Who are we going to keep here, and who are we going to send away?"

Harry said, "What are your thoughts? I haven't even considered it."

"Depends. What are your plans when the mission is complete? Are you going to stop at the grave site?"

"Yes, I am. You'll be there, of course. And Meeka. I'd like to bring Christa, too. I think it would be good for her to support her friend."

"That's it?" Mike said.

"Well, I think Jofre and Iván should be there. You know, in case. If Bill comes back from across the field and he's happy, we can send him on to Djibouti. Sammy can inspect the Twin over the next couple of days just because that will keep him happy, and then he can join Bill in JIB."

"That leaves Ziv, Sasha and Barbara and our comrade for the operation. As far as Carlos Borrajo, I don't know what to expect. He could be with Viza as a second traitor."

"I'm not sure I like leaving Meeka and Christa all alone at the hotel until we're ready to leave. I want to have Ziv stay with them until we give the okay by radio."

Mike said, "Are you prepared for the trail of bodies Ziv will leave behind if anyone tries to harm our girls?"

"Neither you nor I would have it any other way."

28

Harry Delaney **took** out the photos Meeka had taken inside the gold refinery. The school project story worked, and they let the girl look almost everywhere. He scanned them, looking for something he was pretty sure wasn't there.

Christa came up behind him, curious, and looked over his shoulder. "Dad? What are those small dark things? They all look the same, kind of like those chocolate mints without the wrapper. They're not square, though."

Harry examined the photo more closely. "Hmm. You're right, dear. Do you think you could find Meeka and bring her here? I have something I need to ask her. You'd better bring Mike, too."

If what he saw in the picture was true, there was no way they could use the refinery for anything.

While he waited, he looked through the rest of Meeka's pictures one more time. None stood out so much as the one he had set aside. If Meeka confirmed it, and Mike backed her up—well, so much for getting their gold refined for an easy shipment home.

Mike and Meeka arrived with Christa.

Harry held out the picture for them to look at. "Meeka, when you took that one, was there anyone in the room?"

"No. It was empty. The chaperon was talking with someone. While I waited, I looked into the room and noticed those squares. I thought they looked like chocolates without the chocolate on the outside."

"Check the color, Mike. What do you think?"

"Bronze? Not copper. It's too dull." He took the photo from Harry for a better look. "There's some kind of printing on them. Does anyone have a magnifying glass?"

"Come on, Christa. Let's go to the lobby and ask if they have one," Meeka said. The girls hurried off, and soon they returned with a small magnifying glass. Meeka handed it to her father.

"What do you see, Mike?" Harry asked.

Mike brought the loupe to his eye using a method an old geologist once taught him. He looped his finger through the metal cover and bent his thumb to hold it against the edge of his eye. He brought the photo close until it came into focus through the glass. He scanned the brownish-colored "mints", as Meeka called them. "It's not printing, exactly. Engraving, maybe? I can't make it out. Here, Harry. You look."

Harry examined the photo just as carefully. "Do you remember reading that news story? The gold was only gold on the outside. The bars were a mix of what? Copper, tin, zinc and nickel— if I remember right. Only the outside—the wrapping—was gold. It looks as though our gold refinery is nothing more than a scam for the plane we're expecting. They're going to steal the cash before we can get to it."

"Maybe we can sidetrack our competition into thinking we used the refinery for some gold of our own. If they decide on easy pickings, fool's gold is a better bet for them than our own gold." He turned to Meeka. "This picture here. What can you tell me about it?" Harry handed it to the girl. "Do you remember anything else about this room?"

"Oh yes. The woman I was with stopped to talk to one of the workers. I got bored waiting, so I walked down the hall and went into that room. When the woman realized I was missing she yelled my name and came running down the long hall after me."

The two men looked at one another.

"The woman was really upset. She dragged me out and closed and locked the door."

"Sounds about right, Mike. I think we have the start of our fake gold. All we have to do is buy some of it. I think we need to go to the refinery with Iván and Jofre. We'll make them an offer they can't refuse."

Already Mike's wheels were turning. "We could salt the Twin with some of that fake gold. Make whoever wanted inside think they were getting the spoils, so to speak. We better warn Ziv. She won't be a happy camper if we don't."

"If Carlos was a part of the plan with Edouard to rob us, it just might make him think he found the mother-lode. That'll get him off our backs as he makes good his getaway. It'll be a bonus if we find out there's more than the pair of them."

"The only problem is the parcel we've got under wraps," Mike said. "You know, in case."

"You did good work on that school assignment project, Meeka," her father said. "They bought your story, and you returned with the goods, so to speak. I'm proud of you."

"We all are, Meeka. You make a good spy," Harry said. "You probably saved us a lot of work and even more money."

Harry left to track down Ziv in her room and knocked on the door. When she opened it, he explained the plan regarding the fake gold they would buy and put on the Twin. How they hoped it would draw out Carlos and anyone else he was working with against them.

"You'll need to let them walk away with it, Ziv. Don't put your life in danger by any stretch. Once they open the box and see all those shiny gold bars staring up at them, they'll think they got the prize. In fact, they'll have only a few ounces. Allow them to take out the trash, so to speak." He paused. "And one more thing. Don't put your life or our transport out of here in danger."

"Very well. I will relieve Iván."

"You did a good job, Ziv. If you weren't there, who knows what condition our airplane would be in?"

Bill, Sammy and Ziv took a taxi to the freight office, then made their way to the Twin.

Harry made his way back to the palapa, where Iván had returned from standing in for Ziv at the plane. Jofre and Mike were waiting for him.

"One more plan for us, Iván." Harry showed the two men the photo Meeka had taken. "Those look remarkably like gold bars, minus the gold, don't you think?"

"I agree." Iván passed the picture to Jofre. "What is it you want us to do?"

"I need security for a little scheme I've been working on. I want to buy some of those bars in that picture. I have the gold. I'll use it to put some icing on the cake, so to speak. I want you two to provide some muscle to let that so-called refinery know I mean business." Harry paused before going on. "Then we'll haul the fake gold to the Twin in a nice-looking box and see what happens from there."

Jofre asked, "What about Ziv? Does she know?"

"Yes. I already talked to her about it. She'll allow Carlos and whoever else shows up to take away the prize."

Iván asked, "So you think the refinery people are in on the gold scam?"

"There's no doubt now that Mike and I have seen that picture. The refinery is producing the fake gold as we speak. The only thing I'm left wondering is how much hard cash is going to be on that plane when it arrives. Oh, and how much it's going to cost us to get a piece of the fake action, so to speak."

Harry left to call the refinery to make an appointment. He advised them he would be arriving with his security team. When he hung up, he approached the hotel's front desk and the man behind it.

"I need access to a nice car or a van. Do you think you could help us out?" Harry asked, as he reached into a pocket and pulled out a wad of bills.

"Of course, Mr. Delaney. You may use my car. It is the black Audi in the parking lot."

Harry collected the keys and arrived at the gold refinery in style, driven by Iván and overseen by Jofre in the passenger seat. The car halted at the gate, and was admitted by a guard. The gate groaned closed behind them. They were greeted by the same man Harry had met yesterday during their tour of the facility.

"Follow me to my office, gentlemen. We can talk in private there."

When Harry and his men exited the man's office, he had the deal he wanted, and it only cost him a cool thousand dollars. Satisfied, he made his way to the Audi with Iván and Jofre. "Do you think we're going to be able to make this work when we return later tonight for the pickup?"

"If they don't try to screw us," Jofre said. "How many ways can they do that?"

"I guess we'll find out." Harry waved to the security at the gate as they pulled out of the compound. "We still have two days to go. Is anyone else bored by all this waiting around? The only thing different for us is we have a nice resort to return to rather than canvas."

"Well, I don't think Ziv was bored," Jofre said. "Nor were we when she wouldn't or couldn't answer her walkie-talkie. But we're definitely moving up in the world, wouldn't you say?"

"We can do it, Harry," Iván said. "We have to do it. It would be a shame to have you and Mike come all this way for nothing but fake gold. Even worse is that you did it on our word."

29

When **Harry and** his bodyguards returned from the visit to the gold refinery, he sent them off to call everyone to a meeting. With everyone in attendance, he handed off the photo Meeka had taken. "Cast your eyes over that. Were it not for Christa's new-fangled camera, we'd be pounding sand with what little gold resources we have left."

He waited until everyone had a look before going on. "If you can't tell what you're looking at, it's actually fake gold bars—minus the gold plating." The photo made its way around the room again, this time with nods or words of recognition.

"I think we stumbled on the refinery that manufactures the fake gold bars that got busted in Zambia. From what I remember reading, the false gold was a mixture of copper, nickel, tin and zinc. Iván? Jofre? Do you have anything to add?

Iván said, "We read the same articles you did, Harry. What you say about the metals is true to the best of my memory. Jofre? What do you think?"

"It's true," Jofre said. "I wondered about that, too. Now here we are, in the same situation. Harry, if I may?" He stood up to address the group.

"Neither Iván nor myself flew all the way to Canada to convince Harry and Mike to go on a wild goose chase. From what we were told by men we trusted with our lives in the past, there was money to be made with just one of those airplanes. If only we knew where the next would land, since the newspapers blew the thieves' cover. Well, here we find all of us, in this thing to the very end. I am not prepared to give up yet."

Iván stood to join his comrade. "I agree with Jofre. We are in it now. We know an aircraft full of money is arriving in what, two days? I think we learned with Meeka's picture and our refinery visit that someone will be exchanging fake gold for cash. Why do we not take some of that cash? You know, for travel expenses?"

The gathering laughed.

Iván went on. "I'm sure I don't need to speak for Ziv, even though she is not here. I bet she would like a reward for spending all of the resort vacation time Harry and Mike promised her inside one of Mike's old airplanes, would she not?"

The group laughed again.

Mike stood up.

"Come on, you two. The Twin Otter isn't that old. Is it?" He looked at Harry. "Harry would know. He's been flying it for decades in one country or another."

"Good grief, Williams, you make it sound like the airplane is older than I am. Iván and Jofre are right. We're here now. The bribes are in place. Ziv is back in the Twin, waiting to see if Viza, the traitor, was a one-off, or if Borrajo, his partner, was involved, too."

He lowered his voice. "Later I'll be returning to the refinery with my two valued bodyguards to pick up some of that fake gold covered in our actual gold. We're going to take it out for Ziv to babysit along with the Twin. If anyone at the refinery blabs about it, someone will show up to grab it. Ziv is going to let them take it, providing her life isn't threatened. If it is, all bets are off."

Sasha said, "So you think the refinery could be the source of the fake gold? If it is, and if Borrajo knows, he wouldn't want the fake, would he? Why would he bother with fake gold?"

"What else is there? We have Meeka's picture. That pretty much tells the story," Harry said. "And with my visit to drop off some gold for them to coat some of those lovely-looking 'mints', as Meeka calls them, well, take it from there. The refinery, at the least, is guilty as hell."

Mike said, "I really hope Carlos isn't a part of this. He was a good man in the past. We trusted him with our lives."

Harry looked around the room. "I'm seeing a group of people who want to keep up the work. Am I wrong? Does anyone want to pull out?" He waited, then said, "Good. We're still in this together, and damn the consequences."

He checked his watch. "It's time for me and my bodyguards to head over to the refinery." "Our gold bars should have cooled down by now."

He led the men to the borrowed Audi.

"It's now or never, gentlemen."

The three men waited until dark to haul the boxes of gold across the field to the Twin Otter parked on the grass. When Ziv answered their radio call in the affirmative, they knocked on the door. She raised it and looked out.

"Beware of men bearing gifts, someone said. If it weren't for you guys, I'd be wary. Harry, Bill has checked the hardware to his satisfaction. He said to let you know he's gone on to Djibouti and anxiously awaits the arrival of all of us safely—complete with the prize or not."

Harry nodded. "That's one more thing off our checklist. So you know, Sammy is going to show up to go over the plane to make sure she's ship-shape for our getaway. If the man surprises you, don't kill him, okay? We need him."

"For shame, Harry. I haven't yet killed anyone I liked. Not so far, anyway. Is that the gold?"

"Yes, it is. We think the refinery is the weak link in all of this. If Borrajo shows up to steal the fake gold, we'll know he's not a part of the refinery give-away. It's someone else."

Jofre said, "We brought you some fresh fruit and juice and ice courtesy of Meeka and Christa. They're concerned about you out here all alone. Meeka sent you some of her famous fresh chai, too, and some roti."

"Tell them I'm fine. But Harry, when you promise a woman a nice resort vacation, don't make her stay in the back of a Twin Otter that isn't going anywhere soon."

"I'm sorry, Ziv. The reward will be coming soon enough. It's only another day or so according to the plan. Once we're done here, you'll be flying commercial with Sasha and Barbara back to Djibouti."

The men hoisted the box into the cargo hold. "Let Carlos or whoever it is take it away. We only want to see who shows up, remember?"

"No problem." Ziv rustled through the grocery bag the men dropped off for her. "Don't forget to say thanks to Christa and Meeka."

Harry located Sasha relaxing in a beach chair beneath an umbrella. "We need to talk, dear."

"What is it now, Harry? Has something changed we need to know about?"

"Not really. I've got my normal nerves. I'm sure Mike does too. And Iván and Jofre as well. But no. It's about Meeka and Christa. I've been thinking."

"Oh-oh. Now what?"

"Well—" Harry hesitated. He wasn't sure how to approach Sasha about the subject of the two girls. "Mike and I have already talked it over." Right off the bat he knew that wasn't the way to broach the subject. "I mean—"

She smiled at him. "Just spit it out, Harry. I can take it."

"Mike and I would like you and Barbara and Ziv to fly commercial into Djibouti."

"We already figured that out. The Twin will be overloaded at best. I don't feel like flapping my arms to get us airborne and over the mountains. Neither does Barbara. And Ziv missed out on her resort vaycay, don't you know, thanks to that dimwit Viza."

"We'll make it up to Ziv. That isn't what I want to talk to you about. Mike and I are taking Meeka to visit her mother's resting place on the way to JIB. I'd like Christa to come with us. They're good friends, and I think it's important for our daughter to share Meeka's grief."

"I take it Jofre and Iván will be with you, in that case." She looked at her husband. "Are they going to be with you?"

"Yes."

"Then you have my blessing. I agree it's important for Christa to be there for her friend. I wouldn't want it any other way. However..."

Harry grimaced. *There it is. There's always a however with these women ever since*

Mike and I had hooked up with them on the Baja. "Yes?"

"As you well know, if anything should happen to our daughter or to Meeka or to you or Mike, the survivors, meaning Barbara and I, will skin you all alive and hang you to go bad in a Djibouti abattoir. Do I make myself clear?"

30

Meeka overheard **Ziv's** radio call. Her friend was under attack. She pulled on her clothes and went to the closet for the shotgun. She loaded both barrels and put four more shells in her pocket before heading off to knock on Iván's and Jofre's doors.

At each of the doors, she yelled, "Ziv called on the radio. She is in trouble."

The doors opened. Both men were there, their suppressed H&K MP5s ready to do battle.

As Meeka turned away, Iván said, "Where do you think you are going?"

Harry and Mike had joined them in the corridor. They too were prepared to do battle.

"Meeka," Mike addressed his daughter. "I think it would be better if you stay here with Sasha and Barbara and Christa. Stay by the radio. We'll call to let you know, all right?"

She only nodded.

As the men hurried off across the highway toward the Twin, Harry said, "Did you hear that? It's a suppressed HK whispering Ziv's name."

They arrived too late.

Three bodies lay at the entrance to the Twin Otter's cargo door. A fourth almost made it inside before Ziv had dispatched him, too. She pushed the man to the ground with a boot.

The men arrived in time to hear the thump as he landed.

Mike bent to turn the bodies over. "Hand me your flashlight, Ziv." She did, and he aimed the light at each one. "Have a look, guys. Doesn't this one look familiar? He works at the resort. In fact, I think it's his car we borrowed to go to the refinery to place our order."

"Merde," Iván said. "We better get back to the hotel, Jofre."

After the men left to help Ziv, Meeka knocked on each of the doors to alert everyone to what was happening across the field. The women and Sammy gathered in the hotel lobby with one of their radios. All were armed. Even Sammy had hauled out his trusty AK-47.

The garbled radio transmission was barely readable. "Something about a hotel employee," Sammy said.

Sasha said, "Harry borrowed one of their cars—an Audi, I think—to go to the gold refinery with Iván and Jofre when he placed our order. Maybe the lender thought he could get rich off the back of our gold."

"I'll go take a look," Sammy said. "The car might still be in the lot."

"I'll go with you," Barbara said. "Just in case, as Mike and Harry like to say." The pair advanced through the lobby doors into the parking lot. Above them, a business jet flashed its landing lights. The runway lights flicked on. The plane touched down. Thrust reversers engaged and runway lights were extinguished.

Barbara said, "We better call Harry. That might be the plane we're waiting for, Sammy."

The pair rushed inside to the walkie-talkie. Mike took the call on the other end. "You're right. It's taxiing toward us now. Holy shit. We're not ready for this tonight of all nights. We've already got a mess to clean up at the Twin."

Over the jet engine whine of the taxiing plane, Sammy said, "Too late. We're into it now. We'll figure something out at this end." He turned to the women. "All right. It's go-time. That was our plane. Get your bags packed. We're doing it right now, ready or not."

Sammy returned to the parking lot and an old deux chevaux. He reached beneath the dash to pull out wires, recognized it was already hot-wired, and turned the ignition switch. The engine caught on the first try. He steered toward the resort's front door. The women and girls were already waiting.

"Where're your bags?"

Barbara yelled, "We don't have any bags. We're ready. Let's go. Right frigging *now*, Sammy!" The women piled aboard, packing three in the back and one in the front. Barbara looked around the ancient deux chevaux.

"Classy car." She spied the shifter sticking out of the dash. "You drove one before?"

Sammy jerked the gearshift and started the car toward the airport. He glanced at Barbara. "In case you forget, you're going to have to leave your guns in the car. They won't let you on the plane to Djibouti with them."

From the back seat, Sasha said, "Sammy, maybe we could circle around the Twin to see how the guys are making out. We have all these weapons. We might as well put them to use, right?

Sammy glanced in the rear-view mirror. "If anything happens to any of you—"

Barbara pointed. "Turn here, Sammy! The terminal turnoff is coming up."

Sammy cranked the wheel. The ancient Citroën navigated the turn graciously. He doused the lights and continued on past the passenger entrance to the Twin Otter's parking spot.

As the Citroën's doors exploded, Barbara called out. "Need any help?"

Meeka and Christa jumped out of the car, ran for the Twin Otter and jumped on board.

Harry yelled, "Yeah. Get your asses over to that lopsided airplane with the blown tire and guard the thing," Harry instructed. "We don't have all the money on board yet. When we're done, we'll need a distraction. Set fire to it and then clear out. We'll see you in Djibouti."

"Oh! One more thing. Tell Sammy we didn't have time for an inspection," Harry said. "We'll be stopping in Dhobley for fuel.

He knows where it is if he has to come and get us. He's been there before with me."

The starter-generator whined on the Twin Otter's number one engine. It spooled up and ignited with a whump as the start sequence took over and jet-fuel ignited.

31

Christa and Meeka belted in behind Harry and Mike in the cockpit. They made sure to tap their fathers on the shoulder to let them know.

Iván and Jofre finished throwing the bags and bundles of cash out of the business jet's door. Sammy, Barbara, Sasha and Ziv toted it to the Twin Otter's open cargo door and tossed it aboard.

As Christa and Meeka moved to unfasten their seat belts, Mike yelled at them to stay in their seats. "Iván and Jofre are coming with us. They'll do that."

Reluctantly, the girls obeyed.

In the dim light, Iván and Jofre finished tossing bags on board the plane. Iván walked past the bags filled with cash and the girls on his way to the cockpit.

"We're good, Harry. Sammy is driving the women to the terminal. The pogo stick and the load is on board. The door is closed. Cargo netting has been secured."

Harry advanced the throttles and the Twin Otter bumped over the grass-covered parking area beside the cargo-jet offices.

Mike turned to Iván. "What happened to your shirts?"

"We took them off and threw them into the fire."

An orange glow reflected off the terminal windows.

"So we've got three women and Sammy running around the terminal building naked?"

"Merde. Non." Iván pulled at his white t-shirt. "We thought we should get rid of our uniforms since we're traveling. They'll be looking for the people with the fancy shirts who took over the resort hotel. There is no one for them to find."

"You better belt in," Mike told him. "It's going to be a bumpy take-off. Once we get airborne I'll come back and help you adjust the load for our best weight and balance."

Harry looked left and called, "Clear". Mike looked right and did the same. Mike backed up Harry's hands with his own on the throttles. Harry's feet stood on the brakes. The Twin PT-6 engines whined in complaint. When both engines reached peak power, Harry released the brakes and the plane accelerated down the Entebbe taxiway.

"Did you dial in maximum takeoff flaps?"

"Yes, Captain. I dialed in takeoff plus a hair more for fortune."

Harry grinned. "You left out the 'good'."

"We don't need good, Captain. We have a fortune on board. It's all good."

Harry wasn't so busy he couldn't pull the black notebook out of his pocket. He flipped through it one-handed before he found the page. "We'll pick up fuel in HCDB. It's almost a straight shot of 517 nautical. Do you think you can program all that glass in front of us to avoid the hills standing in our way?"

Mike dialed in Dhobley's ICAO airport code. The nav system came to life as the available en route airports and their elevations, radio frequencies and field lengths came up on the screen. He looked up in time to witness Harry unfold the magnetic compass from the center post dividing the two front windscreens. "You going old-school on us now, Delaney?" he asked.

"Not really. Just checking the numbers." He grinned across at his partner.

Meeka reached around the divider to tap her father's shoulder. "Can we go and help Iván and Jofre now, Father?" she asked.

Mike said, "Give me ten minutes and all three of us will go back to help, okay?" He said nothing about how their seating position was helping to balance the load. "Let Iván and Jofre work on their own for now."

Harry worked the trim wheel on the Twin. "I think I've just about got it figured out, First Officer Williams, what do you think?"

"I think you don't need me to tell you anything about a Twin Otter's flight characteristics. Let me know when we can go back and help the guys reposition the load. Our girls are eager to help, too."

Harry looked over the gauges in the dim cockpit lighting. "Our altitude is good. Our temps are good. Our pressures are good. I'm good. I'll be better when I hear news the women are on a plane out of Entebbe."

"You and me both, partner. You and me both. You can send one of the girls back to help the guys. Just one, okay?"

Mike called to Christa. "You can go back now. Your dad has everything under control."

Christa unfastened her belt and walked to the back of the cargo compartment with Iván and Jofre. Harry fine-tuned the trim to make the weight adjustment.

"You can go back in a bit, okay, Meeka?"

The girl nodded and grinned.

"Mike. Dig into my flight bag and see if you can find a 1:500,000 chart, would you? I know I put two or three in. It's just for backup. I don't trust these gauges."

"Next thing you know you'll be tapping the panel. If you do, you want to watch out you don't break any of that glass, Harry."

Mike handed Harry the aviation chart. He recognized an old, faded Michelin road map of East Africa in Harry's flight bag. He pulled that out, too. "You still have that thing?"

"You know I do. You just found it. And I know you kept yours, too. They were our trail maps, remember? There were no roads to speak of, but the caravan trails were marked for sure."

Mike grinned, then stood and called to his daughter. "Come on, Meeka. We need to check the weight and balance back there." He led Meeka to the back where he surveyed the work Iván and Jofre had already done to distribute the bags of cash. "Need some help, guys?"

"There is more than I ever thought we would see, Mike," Iván said. "There were plenty of metal boxes on board the jet, too. We left those behind. I tested one. It was heavy. I don't think it was gold, though."

"Probably just as well. We have all the weight we need for now. We can use full fuel with no problems weight-wise." Mike bent to help redistribute the heavy bags. "Meeka, you can drag some of these up to that window." He pointed. "You, too, Christa. You can help."

Christa tested the weight of a bag. "They're heavy, Uncle Mike."

"Yes they are. That's a good thing, don't you think?" Mike winked at Iván and Jofre. "You can get Meeka to help you."

Under Mike's direction, the crew finished making the changes to the weight and balance of the Twin Otter by redistributing the heavy bags. Jofre and Iván tightened and secured the webbing to keep their precious cargo in place in case they encountered problems en route.

The landing and refueling operation at Dhobley's desert strip went as expected. Iván and Jofre remained out of sight. Harry's old friend, Yuusuf, showed up on time. With pleasantries dispensed with and old times laughed at, the refueling operation from Yuusuf's 55-gallon drums and his electric pump went smoothly. Harry paid Yuusuf in cash. He insisted on leaving a little something extra for Yuusuf's wife. She had sent food to the airport for Harry and his men.

With the operation complete, Mike closed and locked the cargo door while Harry started the engines.

"We've got 540 nautical to our next fuel stop," Harry said.

Mike said, "That sounds like Galkayo."

"I think my first officer has been in these parts before. Do you think Meeka might have anyone she wants to see in our old stomping ground before we head to the desert to visit with her mother?"

"I'll ask her a little later. The girls look like they're ready for a nap after all the local food. Iván and Jofre are right beside them. The pair of them are dozing off already."

"What? Those beggars must be getting old on us. Once we get going, I'm going to steal Christa's camera and take a picture for posterity and blackmail."

Harry did better than that. He took four pictures. He would relish presenting one to each of them in Djibouti.

32

The **Galkayo refuel** went off as scheduled. It appeared as though the farther they got from Uganda and Entebbe, the less hazardous their surroundings were. If not for the colorful shirts they wore, it would have been a clean getaway. For those who flew commercial out of Entebbe to Nairobi and then Mogadishu, there were no problems. Sammy and the women had thrown their shirts into the burning airplane they left on Entebbe's tarmac.

Mike said, "They want to see us in the office, Harry."

"Who's they?"

"I think it's the airport manager. He says the police want to talk to us about something or other."

"All right. Round up our passengers and be sure to remind them we were on safari in Nairobi before school starts. We'll see if the powers-that-be will swallow it, hook, line, and sinker."

"A fishing idiom in the middle of a desert? You're stretching credibility, Harry."

"Well, it wouldn't be the first time, now, would it? For either of us."

Harry gathered the prepared paperwork from his flight bag. It consisted of receipts and photos and letters. It included everyone's passports with appropriately-dated entry and exit stamps. "If this guy doesn't let us out of here before the police arrive, we might be in trouble."

Mike was right about the airport manager wanting to speak with them. He complimented them on their colorful shirts. He smiled at the girls and ignored them. Then he began with his questions. "Where are you coming from? Why were you there and for how long? Did you report at immigration and customs when you entered the country? Are you importing anything into Somalia?"

One by one, Harry responded to the questions, slowly and carefully. He presented the appropriate paperwork as he explained. He told the manager about the survey operation out in the desert to the north, and that it was where they were proceeding. The bottom of the stack of papers concealed a small canvas bag.

The official nodded. He consulted the sheaf of papers while appearing to be deep in thought. When he reached the last page, he flipped it quickly to cover the revealed bag. He hesitated, considering his next move. Finally, he stamped everyone's passport and handed everything back. "You are free to go."

They didn't waste time getting back to the Twin Otter. Harry flipped on the master power switch and checked his fuel levels. Satisfied, he stuck his arm in the back and circled two fingers. "We're good to go. Close us up."

He began taxiing to the strip on one engine until he got number two going. At the intersection to the strip, he poured on the power. The Twin made its way slowly into the blue sky. He was on his way north, 200 kilometers to the next landing.

Harry glanced at Mike. "Let Meeka know we're almost there."

Mike got out of the right seat and nudged his daughter. "Harry wants you to know we're almost with your mother. Go up front and take my seat, dear. I'll stay back here with the poor people." He squeezed her shoulder and smiled.

Harry grinned. "It's about time you showed up, Meeka. I thought you might have stayed behind in Galkayo with old friends."

"I have no old friends in Galkayo, Mr. Harry. They are all gone now, just as I am gone, too"

"I understand perfectly. Take a seat and buckle up while I talk us in."

Harry set descent power and the Twin Otter settled into the glide attitude he wanted. The desert landing strip lay in front of them. The intervening years hadn't been kind. In places, it was overblown with sand. He pointed out the front windscreen. "There's the old strip. Can you see it?"

Meeka strained against her seat belt.

"Loosen it off. It's all right. You'll be with your mother soon, Meeka."

The girl stood to look out the window, careful not to disturb the flight controls. "I see it." Satisfied, she sat back and tightened her belt. She watched him work the flight controls.

"I'm going to do a pass beside the strip to be sure it's in good condition for a landing."

The girl's look of excitement turned instantly to one of disappointment.

"Not to worry, Meeka. This is a good airplane. It can land anywhere. I'll get you there, I promise. It just might take us a little longer, is all."

The smile returned to the girl's face.

Harry maneuvered the Twin Otter parallel to the length of the desert airstrip. "If you look out my window now, you'll see her from the air. Do you remember where she is?"

"Yes. I remember. I can see her."

"Good. The strip is in pretty good condition. We can land on it. I'll taxi us back to where you need to be, all right? It's going to be a little bumpy when we get on the ground. Sort of like the boat ride you took on top of all that water."

"I was not scared. I had Christa and Iván and Jofre with me, as I do now."

"I wouldn't be scared with them, either." He gestured out the front windscreen again. "Our flagpole from when your dad and I worked out of this strip is still sticking up."

The short pole leaned at a precarious angle, minus its windsock flag.

Harry allowed the wheels to contact the sand at the last minute. The plane shuddered and he pulled back on the throttles and eased back on the yoke to keep the nose up for as long as possible. As the plane slowed, he advanced the throttles and adjusted pitch for a torque turn and reversed course. He backtracked the Twin and braked with a wing extending over Eloria's grave. It would provide a measure of shade for the duration of Meeka's visit.

Mike opened the cargo door and jumped down. He reached for Meeka and Christa and helped them out. Harry, Jofre and Iván joined them. One of the men hung the pogo stick.

Meeka walked slowly around her mother's grave-site. "It has been a long time, has it not, Mr. Harry?"

"Yes. But we'll fix it for her. And for you. Right, guys?"

Iván and Jofre took a look at their surroundings. The landscape was one they were familiar with. "Dans La légion we worked with lots of stone and rock to build walls and bridges. There is plenty here that can be used, n'est-ce pas? If you would like our help. Even though we did not know her, we would be happy to help honor your mother."

Harry cast a look in Mike's direction. It was the first time Iván or Jofre had mentioned anything of their former occupations.

"I would like that very much. I think I will not return to her place again."

Christa said, "Can I help with the little rocks, Meeka?"

"Yes. You are my friend. I would like that."

33

The men busied themselves hauling the rock Iván and Jofre picked out. They dropped them in the sand. Once they were satisfied, the two men got busy constructing the stone crypt that would honor Meeka's mother.

Mike said, "Meeka, I think there is one last thing we need to do. If it is all right with you, I think we should leave our shirts behind. Do you think we could place them beneath the rock?"

"Yes. I think that would be all right. It is fitting, is it not? The reason that brought us here is put behind us for good now."

Mike took his daughter's hand. "Yes. It is fitting. Were it not for your mother,

Eloria, none of us would be here. She helped get both Harry and me to safety. We were in a terrible situation. Harry was wounded in the shootout at the plane—"

Harry became lost in his memories. It was true. Were it not for Eloria, and Irit and Mike, he wouldn't be here sharing this moment. It was all because of her. He looked up at his comrades, his men, as Mike went on.

"It was thanks to Harry that I learned about you, my daughter. He and Sasha brought you to me, and to Barbara. I will be forever grateful to them for that, Meeka. And to your mother, Eloria, for giving me such a beautiful and wonderful daughter."

Meeka and Christa collected the shirts and carefully folded them before placing them beneath the final rocks to be put in position by Iván and Jofre. When they finished, they stood back to regard their work.

"I think we did a pretty good job, don't you, Meeka? Your mother would be proud that you are here to remember her."

"Yes. I am glad, too. It feels good to have my friends help."

"There's a blanket in the back of the airplane," Mike said. "There's food left, too. I think we deserve a break." Mike retrieved the blanket and spread it beneath the shade of the wing. Meeka and Christa brought out what was left of the food and water and everyone sat for a break.

A gray cloud approached. "Look, everyone. Rain is coming." He looked up to spot the virga, the rain that doesn't land. It appeared first, before the cloud drifted overtop.

Meeka said, "*Roob*. That is the word for rain from a cloud that falls to the ground."

"Watch carefully. When the rain is finished, bright tiny flowers will bloom quickly. Just as quickly, they will shrivel and disappear. Do you remember, Meeka?"

"Yes, Mr. Harry. I remember the flowers when we were here first."

Harry and Mike and Meeka stood beneath the wing as the rain landed. It was barely enough to make a raindrop pattern in the loose sand. Minutes later, the tiny flowers began appearing. Meeka walked out among the blooms, careful not to disturb the short, tiny flowers.

To the west, a cloud of dust drifted skyward to announce something approaching the landing strip.

Harry said, "All right, everyone. It's time to go." By the time everyone was seated and the door was closed, the flowers began disappearing.

"Meeka, would you like to sit up front with me for takeoff? I need a good co-pilot to set my flaps for me."

The girl jumped up and went to sit in the co-pilot's seat beside Harry. The grin on her face was huge as she fastened her seat belt. "I am ready."

Harry handed her the headset and she put it on. He advanced the throttles and the Twin began moving. "Give me 10," Harry said.

Meeka reached for the flap lever and put in the setting.

"You remembered." Harry followed her movement with his eyes as the plane continued down the rough, uneven sand runway. The wings rocked from side to side as the plane traversed the uneven ground.

Harry pulled back the column and the Twin became airborne. He continued straight and level, leaving the power setting in place. Mike tapped him on the shoulder.

"Someone let fly with an RPG just after liftoff. I think we can handle it from the back if you turn us around in time."

Harry nodded, and Mike went aft to open the cargo door. Already Iván and Jofre had the mini-gun positioned and ready. "They're south of the strip. If Harry can keep us at this height, we can put them out of action."

The slipstream rushed into the cargo compartment, making it difficult to be heard. The men donned the headsets Mike handed them. The wind noise was cut, making it easy to hear instructions.

"We're too heavy to put this thing into a pylon turn. I'm going to give you an oval when I get sight of them. Call it, Mike." Harry continued his slow climb to altitude. When he was satisfied, he began positioning the plane, all the while listening to Mike's instructions over the headset.

Meeka poked him in the arm and motioned aft.

Harry said, "No. Stay here. Mike is busy in the back. He won't be up front for a while. There's no need to worry about your mother's place. The men are far from it."

Meeka nodded and continued watching Harry, busy at the flight controls.

Harry said, "All right. I have them, Mike. Tell whoever is manning the gun to get ready."

"Everyone can hear you, Harry."

Iván called to Harry on the intercom. "The bungees are attached. We won't be taking out any parts of your plane."

The mini-gun whirred into action under the capable hands of Jofre. It took him two short bursts to get sighted in on the technicals as they drew closer to the landing strip. Two more bursts took care of the first technical in the line. Another burst took out a truck.

"There's an RPG about to be launched, Jofre."

"I see him." Jofre swung the mini-gun and let fly with another burst. The shooter and his armorer disappeared in a pink cloud.

Mike asked, "Are you sure you've never been behind one of these before?"

"It is easy. Bill gave us both a quick course in Djibouti. I was starting to think we would never use it. Iván? Your turn." Both men grinned as they switched positions.

Iván used the opportunity to clean up what was left of the truck convoy before announcing it was done.

"Thanks, gentlemen. I'm going to do a low-and-slow for Meeka before we head off to Djibouti. Is everyone all right with that?"

There was no response. Everyone in the back went to the starboard windows to look out. Harry dialed in the trim correction for the center-of-gravity adjustment.

Harry turned to look at Meeka. Her face was glued to the window, and she was smiling a huge smile. He gently squeezed her shoulder.

A tear trickled down her face.

"Thank you, Mr. Harry. I will not forget."

34

Harry had Djibouti dialed in on the nav system. The weather was CAVU: ceiling and visibility unlimited. Eyl and the deep blue of the Indian Ocean appeared off the starboard wing briefly before the ocean disappeared as he turned en route. The next water would be the Gulf of Aden. He was climbing above 5,000 feet. The gauges were good. Meeka would be bored. He told her she could go aft if she wanted.

Meeka climbed out of her seat and gave Harry a kiss on the cheek and a huge hug before heading aft to join her friends.

A moment later, Mike settled into the co-pilot's chair and buckled up.

Harry looked at him. "Your daughter just made me the happiest man in the world." He dialed in more power to get the overloaded Twin Otter to altitude faster.

"Before she left she kissed me on the cheek and—"

A loud bang interrupted Harry's description of Meeka's hug. The starboard wing dipped. Mike looked aft out the window to the damaged starboard engine. Flames were coming out the back end. "We lost number two. It looks like compressor stall judging by the flames."

Harry brought up number one's power setting to compensate for the loss of lift caused by the stalled starboard engine. At the same time, he kicked in rudder to compensate as he cut fuel on the stalled engine. The flames trailing the engine extinguished.

Mike called it. "The flames are gone."

The master warning caution switched on. Systems began shutting down.

"We need both engines," Harry said. "We're too heavy for one. Clean up drag and then go for those noisy bells and whistles if you have a minute, Mike."

Mike feathered number two's propellers to reduce drag. "Feathering complete," he said. He pulled circuit breakers to halt the warning horns. Finally, silence reigned in the cockpit.

"Take another look and see if we're still on fire, would you?"

Mike checked out the side window again. "No more orange. Did you set off the fire bottle?"

"No. I don't want to jeopardize the engine any more than it is," Harry told him.

Harry's gaze moved to check the altimeter. Already it was moving in a direction—albeit slowly—that he didn't want to see.

"I'm going to try for a restart before we lose any more altitude." He flipped the start switch. It was dead. "All right. I'm going to dive her to see if I can put some life back into the old girl."

He eased forward on the column. The nose began dropping. Altitude began falling off more rapidly. "Call out my N1, Mike."

Mike called the numbers. "Ten. Twelve. Thirteen. Now!"

Harry activated the fuel lever. Number two whined and slowly came back to life.

Mike brought the propeller blades out of feather and ever so slowly, began increasing pitch.

Harry checked the power gauges. "We have an engine," he announced. "I'll bring her back up slow and steady." He moved his gaze to his altimeter. It was holding.

"I'll go back and let everyone know we're safe and bound for Djibouti. Do you have an ETA I can pass along?"

Harry focused his attention on the glass cockpit. "We'll be another couple of hours. You can tell Jofre he can break out the cards. Speaking of which, are those two planning on crossing at Casablanca?"

"I'll ask, but I suspect so, just like last time. It's their preferred way to get home."

"Good. Christa was asking about Casablanca the last time we were at our kitchen table. She saw the picture of everyone in the back of the DC-3."

"Well, this time, the picture will be taken in the back of my jet. We'll all be dressed normally for a change."

"Speak for yourself, Mike."

It was 2200 hours when Harry finally taxied to park beside Mike's jet on the Djibouti tarmac. Sammy and Bill met the Twin Otter. When the people and the packages had been unloaded, they went to work on the mini-gun.

Sammy noticed the empty canister immediately. "What happened?"

"We encountered a little trouble after we took off from visiting Meeka's mom. She's fine. The outfit that let fly with a couple of

RPGs is no more, thanks to Jofre's and Iván's fine shooting."

"That's good to hear. Anything else I should know about?"

"Well, there is one small thing."

Sammy waited, wondering what would be coming next.

"I had a compressor stall on number two. It was hot, and as you saw, we were overloaded. I managed to get her restarted. She behaved pretty good all the way here, too, but I had to nurse her along."

"The starter I borrowed wasn't very reliable. You should talk to your spares department about that. Did Mike mention anything about a new engine?"

"No, but I think he was tallying the cost for the remainder of the flight. I'm going to have to remind him he can take it out of the luggage if he wants to pay cash."

"Yeah, I'm going to leave that to you. He might be a bit sensitive about it."

"Just so you know, Sammy, we'll be heading home through Casablanca. Iván and Jofre—

Sammy held up his hands. "Just like last time. Say no more. I hear you."

"I'd like to send Bill home ahead of everyone. Do you want to come with us or fly home from here?"

"I think I'd like to go with you guys if that's all right. Christa is going to be pleased as punch. I overheard her telling Sasha about Casablanca and the old picture of all of us in back of the DC-3."

"We're going first class this time, Sammy. Mike is going to take us in the jet. There'll be no stopping at sand beaches to see the sights like last time."

"Thank goodness for that."

Harry joined Mike, Jofre, and Iván, separated from the group and already deep in discussion. "Are you guys talking about what I think we need to talk about?"

"Yeah, we are," Mike said. "I think we should consider storing our payday in Spain. What do you think?"

Harry had already considered it. He'd spoken to Sasha, and she had agreed. "But that means we'll have to place a lot of trust in Jofre and Iván.

Harry had responded, "We've already put the lives of our children and ourselves into their care. We need to pull our heads out and make the move we talked about."

Harry looked at Mike. "I'm good with it if you are. Sasha says yes, too." Then he smiled at Jofre and Iván. "I think you might find yourselves with some competition in the café business back home once we get set up."

Iván and Jofre high-fived. "We can take it. We'll be waiting to hear from you."

Mike said, "Now that we've settled that, when Sammy and Bill are finished, we'll be taking off for Casablanca. Do you guys have any complaints about that?"

"None in the slightest. We have already checked. Our comrades are waiting with papers and a boat. We are going to be sailors again. It's too bad Christa and Meeka can't join us on this trip. It won't be as much fun without them."

"Then you'd better tell them yourself," Mike said. "They'll be pleased as punch to know they're going to be missed by you old desert sailor softies."

M eeka and Christa were pleased their two favorite traveling companions singled them out for praise. Christa said, "We won't forget you, Iván. You too, Jofre. We had so much fun, from the elephants and buying you ginger ale in the bar and our road trip and our boat trip and—"

"And for helping me take care of my mother," Meeka said. "I saw your tattoos. I am flattered."

Iván smiled. "So you recognized the person, did you?"

Meeka said, "Yes. I am sorry I gave you such a hard time back home. If I had known—"

"Did you do what you thought was correct for the time?"

"Oh yes, and I would do it again if I did not know you now. It is my duty with Harry. He is the one who found me and brought me home to be with my father."

Jofre said, "Well, you did your duty very well. As you can tell by the ink, we are proud to know you. You too, Christa. We will miss both of you on our boat trip home. It will not be so much fun for us. Did your father tell you we are all going to Casablanca?"

"Oh yes," Christa replied, excited. "I saw the old picture of you in the back of the DC-3. Do you think you will miss it?"

Iván grinned. "Not on your life. We like these modern times."

35

A Citroën sedan pulled up to the crew gathered around the airplanes. Renaud got out to greet Harry and Mike. He nodded curtly to Iván and Jofre, whom he knew from another life. "I am glad to see you are all back safely. How did it go?"

"We accomplished what we set out to do. Any more than that I can't say."

Mike grinned. "And if we did, it would only be lies anyway, Gilbert. You know that."

The capitaine looked at Harry. "Your wife, Sasha. She has the MAC50, does she not?"

"Yes, she does. It has stood by her well. Would you like it back?"

"Oh, no. Not at all. I see she also keeps her spare magazine in her brassiere. I must remember to tell my wife. She is the owner of the twin to that one, and she does the same."

"This is the first time it has seen action after all these years, Gilbert. I think Kari would be proud to know."

"I think she would too. How did the borrowed armament perform? I heard talk of an empty canister coming back."

"It worked one hundred percent. I'm glad we had it. And speaking of that, I'd like to provide a small finder's fee to you for helping us. We couldn't have pulled this off without your help."

Mike dug into a bag and pulled out a wad of cash. He slipped it into a paper bag before approaching Capitaine Renaud and handing it over. "All of us thank you for every bit of your help. I think your wife will appreciate the gift. It might help her to make a decision, but of course I know nothing about such things. We all know sometimes they need a little push and a bit of a cushion, so to speak."

"Transport is on its way to pick up the armament. It won't be sitting on the tarmac for long. It was good to see all of you one more time, mes amis. I don't expect it will happen again soon."

"You're right. The old days are gone for all of us now."

"I have two small gifts for each of your girls. I cannot make the claim that they are from me. They will find out when they open them." Renaud waved and drove off.

The transport for the mini-gun arrived, and it was loaded and hauled off.

"I'm going to order up a new PT-6 for that airplane," Mike said to Harry. "I'll check with my chief accountant, but I think we can afford it. Let's get aboard our DC-3 replacement and find out how she performs en route."

Harry said, "All aboard that's getting aboard. Next stop, Casablanca."

"Don't forget to do a head count before we close the door," Mike said. "If we leave anyone behind, we'll really be deep into it with all these women."

Meeka and Christa carefully unwrapped the fancy packages Renaud had left for them. "Look, Dad. It's a movie. It's called *Casablanca*. Meeka got the same one."

Sasha said, "Well now. It looks like we're going to have a movie night when we get home. Who's going to be buying the popcorn?"

The girls weren't finished with their presents.

"Look, Christa. A card. Did you get one too?"

Christa nodded, and together they opened the small envelopes.

"Mom. It's from Jofre. Meeka? Who is yours from?"

"It's from our friend Iván."

"We called Renaud and asked him to pick up the gifts," Jofre explained. "His wife did the lettering on the cards. I think Iván and I, how do you say, made a hit?"

Sasha and Barbara got out of their seats and proceeded to hug the grizzled veterans before calling to their daughters.

Iván said, "I think your girls are speechless for the first time."

"Girls, you have thank-you letters to write when you get home," Barbara said. "Don't forget to get addresses."

The blushes from the two men had barely disappeared when Meeka and Christa came over to hug them, too.

Ziv checked the fridge and the microwave before proceeding to the front of the cabin. She stuck her head into the cockpit, confirmed the destination, and closed and secured the cockpit door before taking her seat at the front.

Iván nudged Jofre. "She's a strange one. I'm glad she's on our side."

"It all makes sense now, Iván."

"What do you mean?"

"Harry pays her, right? She's a companion for Meeka. Or a bodyguard. Or both. Ziv is Israeli, like Meeka's mother."

"Why do you say that?"

"Remember the songs Meeka sang under her breath when she was making food for us? You asked about them, and I said it was probably Hebrew. Now I know it to be so. The girl is so protective of Harry. It's a good thing we didn't do anything stupid when she caught us out on the street in front of Harry's place. She would have killed both of us for sure."

Harry exited the cockpit and closed the door behind him. He bent to speak with Ziv.

She got up and walked aft to Iván and Jofre. The pair followed her to the front of the jet, where she unlocked the cockpit door to allow entry. All four of them entered the cramped quarters. Harry took his seat and Ziv secured the door behind them.

"One of the girls found an envelope full of 'pretty paper', as she called it. She didn't know what to do with it since it wasn't cash, so she turned it over to Ziv." Harry held out a piece of paper. His handwritten numbers and dollar signs trailed down the page. Iván took the paper, looked at it, and handed it off to Jofre. Both men whistled before passing it back to Harry.

Harry said, "The only ones who know about this are here in the cockpit. Does anyone have any questions?"

No one did.

"Then here's what I think. Correct me if you have a problem before I finish. We're all partners in this to the end." He hesitated before going on. He held out the envelope and pulled the bearer bonds partway out for the men to see. "There's twenty-five of them in there. All the same denomination. My suggestion is one each for the participants in this crazy scheme. That includes Sammy and Bill and Christa and Meeka, to make a total of, what, eleven?"

Iván and Jofre nodded agreement. "Oui. Onze. Eleven."

"Are you and Iván okay with that, gentlemen?" Harry asked.

"Oui. D'accord. Of course."

"There is one more thing. Call it a finder's fee, if you must. If the pair of you hadn't showed up on Meeka's doorstep, so to speak, none of us would be here now. I'm sure you had your doubts before you got on that airplane in Spain. I had my own when you told us what you wanted to do. And we all had our doubts the further we got into this deal."

He hesitated again.

"There is one extra for each of you. The finder's fee I mentioned. I hope it's enough. Mike has dedicated his business and his aircraft to the undertaking. He'll get the rest of it, if that's acceptable."

Iván and Jofre shrugged. Iván said, "Why not? We cannot disagree. We had our doubts all along, too. Even more when our comrades turned out to be traitors."

"Good. Then there's one more small thing." Harry hesitated and smiled at the two men. "Well, two, actually. And maybe they're not so small. We don't know if the bonds are counterfeit. They could be just like the false gold they were making at the refinery. If that's the case, we're all out for our troubles." He stopped, waiting for a reaction.

Jofre said, "Let me see one, Harry."

He pulled a bond out of the envelope and passed it to Jofre. Jofre ran a fingernail up and down the length. He unscrewed a water bottle, rolled up the bond, and stuck it in the bottle as far as it would go, allowing it to soak. He pulled the paper out and unrolled it and did the same with his fingernail over the wet paper. "It looks good to me. How can we know for sure until we try to redeem them?" He handed the paper back to Harry.

"You said there were two things," Iván said. "What's the second?"

"Mike and I would like to send our families over next summer for a vacation while we try to unload our business on some poor sucker. We're not looking to freeload. We'll put them up in a villa or whatever you call a hotel over there."

"Are we going to have competition for our businesses? We were enjoying a relaxed lifestyle drinking ginger ale and spending free time with our families, you know."

"I'll be sure to send some Canada Dry with them, mes amis. Oh, and Ziv will be going along, too."

Jofre said, "Pas de problème." He grinned at Ziv. "We'll teach her how to bake bread and croissants, n'est-ce pas, Ziv? And of course little Meeka and Christa will make us chai. But without the flies, right Iván?"

MEEKA & CHRISTA
present
Casablanca
POP CORN
POP CORN
MOVIE
Night
CINEMA
CINEMA
SATURDAY START AT 7PM
FREE GINGERALE • FREE POPCORN • DOOR OPEN AT 6PM

About the author

Peter Duke is a Canadian author. He resides and writes in a small college town in the Province of Ontario.

Peter's gypsy spirit has taken him to some strange places in the world, but now he's content to limit his adventures to riding a motorcycle and whatever he might encounter when he's on the road. Consequently, he's worked in bike shops doing odd jobs from planning and putting on rides down Mexico way, taking care of computer networking and security, and to picking up and delivering motorcycles from the L.A. basin to Las Vegas, among other things.

He's ridden over a lot of North America at one time or another from Canada to Mexico, and from Atlantic to Pacific. By far his favorite ride is up and down the length of the Baja Peninsula, where the people are friendly, the sun always shines and it's warm in the winter.

Of everything that he has experienced in his all-too-brief life, Africa is perhaps the greatest enigma. It's a beautiful continent, rich in people, nature and resources, yet poor in all of those areas, too.

pxduke.com

peterxduke@gmail.com

If you enjoyed reading about Harry Delaney, you might like another PX Duke series. Police Detective Jim Nash has a murky back-story in the police department of a major city. Check it out.

Print books

Jim Nash

Jim Nash The Beginning
Gun Crazy
Gun Crazy 2
Gun Crazy 3
Fallen Angels
Last Stop to Nowhere
Revenge is Justice
Escape / Forget Me Not
Wedding Bell Blues / Breakdown
Mexico Time
No Free Ride / Gone
LOBO
Stealing America
Blame It on Djibouti
No Escape
Trouble in Paradise
Nash & Delaney Collide

Harry Delaney Adventures

Dead Reckoning
Lie Cheat Steal
Uncharted
Go-Around
Sand Storm
Harry Delaney Collection

Frank Ross Biker Tales

No Way Out
Bad Girls
Bank Robber Dames

Other

The Last President

Jim Nash Read Order

JIM NASH

Jim Nash The Beginning
Pirate Cay
Thrill Kill Jill
Greetings From Key West
Lost Paradise
No Angels
Mexico Gamble
No Picnic
Fallen Angels
Vendetta
A Girl's Best Friend
Dead End
No Harbor
Dog Days
Startup Blues
Last Stop To Nowhere / The Last Goodbye
Revenge Is Justice
Escape
Wedding Bell Blues
Snap Brim Fedora Caper
Breakdown
Little Girl Lost
Forget Me Not
All The Glitter
Mexico Time
Partners In Crime
Shop Till You Drop
Lobo
No Free Ride
Gone
Stealing America
Blame It on Djibouti
No Escape
Trouble in Paradise
Nash & Delaney Collide

SEASONAL

Trick or Treat
Helping Santa

JIM NASH INVESTIGATES

The Snap Brim Fedora Caper
The Lady in White
The Lady in Yellow

Cover images:

mencism, Pixabay

jason-yoder-9YHiZyN1-PU, Unsplash

schuetz-mediendesign, Pixabay

Ben_Kerckx, Pixabay

soofiatailor, Pixabay